Nice Girls Don't

Caroline B. Cooney

SCHOLASTIC INC.
New York Toronto London Auckland Sydney Tokyo

ISBN 0-590-32846-8

12 11 10 9 8 7 6 5 4 3 2   5 6 7 8 9/8

Printed in the U.S.A.   06

Nice Girls Don't

A Wildfire® Book

WILDFIRE® TITLES FROM SCHOLASTIC

I'm Christy by Maud Johnson
Beautiful Girl by Elisabeth Ogilvie
Superflirt by Helen Cavanagh
Dreams Can Come True by Jane Claypool Miner
I've Got a Crush on You by Carol Stanley
An April Love Story by Caroline B. Cooney
Yours Truly, Love, Janie by Ann Reit
The Summer of the Sky-Blue Bikini by Jill Ross Klevin
The Best of Friends by Jill Ross Klevin
Second Best by Helen Cavanagh
Take Care of My Girl by Carol Stanley
Secret Love by Barbara Steiner
Nancy & Nick by Caroline B. Cooney
Senior Class by Jane Claypool Miner
Cindy by Deborah Kent
Too Young To Know by Elisabeth Ogilvie
Junior Prom by Patricia Aks
Saturday Night Date by Maud Johnson
He Loves Me Not by Caroline Cooney
Good-bye, Pretty One by Lucille S. Warner
Just a Summer Girl by Helen Cavanagh
The Impossible Love by Arlene Hale
A Kiss for Tomorrow by Maud Johnson
The Searching Heart by Barbara Steiner
Write Every Day by Janet Quin-Harkin
Christy's Choice by Maud Johnson
The Wrong Boy by Carol Stanley
Make a Wish by Nancy Smiler Levinson
The Boy for Me by Jane Claypool Miner
Class Ring by Josephine Wunsch
Phone Calls by Ann Reit
Just You and Me by Ann Martin
Homecoming Queen by Winifred Madison
Holly in Love by Caroline B. Cooney
Spring Love by Jennifer Sarasin
No Boys? by McClure Jones
Blind Date by Priscilla Maynard
That Other Girl by Conrad Nowels
Little Lies by Audrey Johnson
Broken Dreams by Susan Mendonca
Love Games by Deborah Aydt
Miss Perfect by Jill Ross Klevin
On Your Toes by Terry Morris
Christy's Love by Maud Johnson
Nice Girls Don't by Caroline B. Cooney

One

"Do you realize," said my best friend Ferris, "that last week I stopped being a daughter and became a disposal problem?"

Ferris used to be practically a poster child for suburban America. You'd see her leaning up against their station wagon, or hugging the golden retrievers, or doing cartwheels on the lawn. On Saturdays she was always raking the maple leaves and rescuing kittens from trees.

"Now, Ferris," I said soothingly. She was getting this pink look around her eyes. She was going to cry. The thing about Ferris was that we had to keep her busy. Make her write that paper, ride that horse. Otherwise, she started thinking about her parents' divorce.

I huffed on the inside of the car window and began drawing my initials on the glass and wrapping them in hearts.

"It's true," said Ferris hollowly. "I'm like

atomic waste. Or rotting oranges. My parents have to find a place to put me where I won't be in their way."

"Now, Ferris," I said, just full of comforting thoughts and useful suggestions.

"I," said Chrissie loudly, "would like another inch. I have been allotted precisely half a foot in which to sit, and although I am slender, petite, and perfectly formed, I am not six inches wide."

Mary Cat made a few scathing remarks about Chrissie's true shape and condition, and we all tried to squeeze over. With four of us jammed into the backseat of Missile's car, this was not easy.

Missile is our gym teacher. Her real name is Miss Lutkenczycki, which was shortened years ago to Miss L, which we turned into Missile. For her birthday we gave her a tiny missile pin, a little scarlet rocket with orange flames. She wears it on her lapel at all the basketball games.

"Nobody is listening to me," said Ferris, in such a sad voice I figured next she'd cough with a terminal lung disease. "Nobody ever listens to me."

"Ferris," said Mary Cat, "all we *ever* do is listen to you. The whole school knows about your divorce problems. You tell anybody who so much as pauses to shift books from one hip to another about your problems."

Ferris glared at her. "You're not listening to me," she said fiercely.

"We're too busy smelling you," said Chrissie. "Ferris, did you take a shower? Anyone who scores nineteen points in one game needs to take a shower."

Ferris defended her odor.

I wrote "Kenny" in my heart, doing him first in script, and then in capitals, and finally in circles, so it came out "nnyKennyKe."

"Tory," said Missile, "would you stop writing on my window?"

I stopped.

"At night when I'm peering around foggy corners and gauging the speed of oncoming moving vans," said Missile, "all I can see are your lopsided hearts."

"Sorry." I tried to erase them with my hand, but this left a fat palm print. I fished around in my duffel bag for my towel — nice and damp and more than capable of washing windows. A stench came from around my feet. It was definitely time to do laundry again. I thought longingly of the boys' team. They get their uniforms supplied fresh each week by the cleaners. They don't even have to take theirs home, let alone wash them.

Chrissie began a dissection of our game. She plans someday to be the most hated woman sportscaster in the nation, and we feel she is well on the way. No one can be as caustic and vicious as Chrissie. "And in the second quarter," she said, "when Tory wouldn't. . . ."

I chose not to hear about how I could have stopped number seventeen from getting that basket by deliberately fouling her. Everybody knew she couldn't shoot free throws. I remembered instead the good parts — like the six points I racked up.

Peggy, in the front seat of the car with Missile, began a flow of her own. I couldn't hear her because of Chrissie, but I knew exactly what she was saying. "In Iowa," she was saying. Peggy moved here two months ago and she wakes up every single morning praying to be in Iowa, and she never is, so she spends the whole day frowning. "In Iowa, we used to. . . . In Iowa, there was. . . . In Iowa we had. . . ."

Iowa gets old in a hurry.

"And then my mother said," Ferris droned on.

"Oh, dear," I said appropriately, and I daydreamed: The stands would be full of screaming, stomping fans, all bused in for our big game. Kenny would be there. Even though it's against the rules, he would have a noisemaker. The ref would have to single him out and yell that he was disrupting the game. Kenny would say, "But that's my girl down there — Tory Travis. I gotta cheer!"

Not likely, I thought, half in the dream, half out.

Kenny is not the cheering type. He is like the line on the graph that goes straight from one side of the chart to the other without a single blip. I mean, we are talking about someone who, when he is completely thrilled, might raise an eyebrow. Not two eyebrows. He doesn't want to go overboard. Just one.

Besides, Kenny goes to the boys' games. There is nearly always a scheduling conflict and if you like boys' basketball (and who doesn't? I love it), then you can't see the girls play, too.

Furthermore, I'm not Kenny's girl. We have gone out three times, count them, three: one movie, one backyard, and one pizza. I have big plans for Kenny and me, but it's kind of like planning to win the state basketball championship. Definitely on the iffy side.

I daydreamed about basketball.

What I yearn for is a radio commentator who yells into the microphone. I love it when their voices boom and crackle.

You know how, in boys' games, they introduce each kid by his nickname? And the boy trots out and beats on his chest, or slaps the hands of the other guys? And the fans applaud and stomp till the bleachers rattle? *And number twenty-three — our oowwnnn Robertson D. "Dusty" Lang!* blares the mike. Scream, scream, stomp, stomp.

We have great nicknames on our team. Nothing as dull as Dusty. We'd sound terrific shouted into a mike. *And noowww — that famous ball hog — Victoria "Tory" Travis! And the one and only Ferris "The Wheel" Cooke! Followed by their brilliant captain, Mary Catherine "Mary Cat" Romney!*

When there really *was* a blare and a shriek outside of my daydream, I nearly fell on the floor of Missile's car.

But it was just the athletic bus going in

5

the other direction carrying the boys' team to their game. They were stopped at one side of the red light and we were stopped on the other. In spite of the rain, they leaned out their windows to yell at us.

Chrissie rolled down her window and stuck her head out in the water and shrieked, "We *won!*" and pulled back in and said, "I swallowed a mouthful of rain."

The boys gave us the high sign. Dusty Lang, who is so tall it makes your eyelids ache locating his face, leaned so far out that the coach began hauling him back in by the belt.

"Good luck!" screamed Chrissie. Missile honked a message of encouragement and their bus passed us, tossing a spray of puddle on Chrissie. Behind them came a bunch of cars: cheerleaders, parents, fans, and girl friends. I strained to see Kenny among them, but his handsome face, with its long, thick brown hair flopping over his forehead, was not there.

I have always adored Kenny. He is so good-looking I truly don't believe it. First, I don't believe anyone can look that good, and second, I don't believe he's taken me out. I knew from the first time I found out that boys date girls that Kenny and I should go together like a happy foot in a comfy old sneaker. And when Kenny asked me out the first time — we were twelve, I think — it should have meant a lifetime of dating. Instead I completely blew it. Even now I cringe, thinking of what I did to him.

We were in the parking lot: dozens of kids converging on their car-pool drivers. Twelve is an uncivilized age for girls. Nobody I knew had ever had a date, asked anybody else to go on one, or seriously considered having one. Dating was something you giggled about or watched high school kids do. You didn't actually commit dating yourself.

So when Kenny said to me, "Tory? You want to go out with me this weekend? To the movies or something?" I didn't know what to do. I was thrilled and embarrassed, confused and excited. My first date! But what to do? How to handle it?

Well, when twelve-year-old girls don't know how to react . . . they giggle.

I can still hear my laugh, pealing out over the pavement, bouncing off car windows, piercing the ears of every kid in our grade. At the top of my lungs I shrieked, "Guess what, you guys? Kenny thinks I'd like to go somewhere with him! In *public!*"

Naturally, everybody fell onto the pavement laughing.

For one shocked moment Kenny stared at me. I remember how his face froze, as if I'd thrown something sharp and hard at it. And then he burst into desperate laughter himself, trying to agree that it was all some crazy joke he'd thought up. Next year when we had the same math class, Kenny got a transfer. I tried to tell myself he wanted a different teacher, but I didn't think that was the reason.

The first day of school this year — the first day of my junior year—Kenny Magnussen sat down next to me in English and borrowed my pencil and on the same first day of school, leaving the building to catch the bus, Kenny Magnussen asked me out for the second time. I didn't shriek, giggle, or send out signals to every witness to burst into laughter. I said, "Oh, Kenny, I'd love to."

Sometimes I just sit and think about what a good year this is. Kenny starting. Basketball going well. Decent grades so far.

I never thought it would happen to me — all good things at one time. My experience was that you have a raft of ordinary aspects to your life: things so acceptable and dull you're hardly aware of them. Maybe one terrific thing — like last year, making varsity. Maybe one bad thing — like last year when my favorite Aunt Cathy divorced my favorite Uncle Mark. But this year, if I made lists, everything would be under *Good* and nothing under *Lousy*.

"What would it be like to be Dusty Lang and have colleges clamoring for your presence?" Mary Cat's voice interrupted my thought.

"That's why Dusty has become such a pill lately," said Chrissie. "All that attention."

"Pill?" snorted Mary Cat. "Listen. Dusty

Lang is such a turkey his parents can't let him out in November."

We groaned together. Ferris wanted to know how Mary Cat could tell turkey jokes when she, Ferris, was in the midst of a crisis.

"In Iowa," said Peggy clearly, "the girls used the athletic buses, too. Nobody had to car-pool."

"If I hear one more word about Iowa," said Ferris, "I am going to have a nervous breakdown."

"I second that," said Chrissie.

Peggy went white but she didn't shut up. "Still," she said, "in Iowa, boys and girls were equal."

"That's just my point," cried Ferris. "My *brother* gets to choose whatever *he* wants. Boarding school. Living with Dad. Living with Mom. Even living with my grandmother. But Ferris? Does she get a choice? No. Ferris has to be a little lady and do what she's told."

In spite of being jammed thigh to thigh with the other girls, I suddenly had this weird sense of losing my balance. At first I thought I was dizzy, and then I decided it was psychological. Came from having to deal with Ferris so much: Ferris, who felt cliffs and chasms all around her. Walk carefully, Tory baby, I thought, there are pits out there.

I am not normally a careful person. Normally I see something interesting and I fling myself into it with every fiber and muscle I have. If I have something to celebrate, I go find somebody to hug — the old lady next door, the cat, a waitress — anybody to share it with.

Once, a girl whose name I refuse even to mention said, "Tory, you're like a Saint Bernard puppy. All feet and tongue. Grow up. Calm yourself." Well, I didn't do it for her (what I would have done for her doesn't bear repeating), but I seem to be doing it for Kenny. With Kenny I have this sense that I have to be casual and relaxed. So that's what I'm teaching myself this year, along with chemistry, English, French, history, and better free throws. I try to emulate Mary Cat, who is a wonderful combination of elegance and jock. I think Mary Cat is very exciting. I cannot imagine why there are not hordes of boys lined up at her door begging for her company. Do you ever go into a room and see all these duds, these complete rejects of girls — and the boys *like* them? And there's somebody terrific, like Mary Cat, alone; and you think, boys are completely inexplicable. They could have Mary Cat, who is perfect, and they date those slobs over there.

Anyway, I am far from perfect and far from calm, so junior year also involves a lot of work on my part.

There was another series of honking behind our car, and this time it was Susannah's mother, good old reliable Mrs. Fargo, driving the rest of the team toward home. Mrs. Fargo was waving like mad and gesturing to the left, where the Burger King loomed up out of the pouring rain like a greasy savior.

"Missile, stop!" yelled Mary Cat and Chrissie. "Stop!"

"No," said our coach flatly. "Mrs. Fargo took every single one of you to the Dairy Queen after the last game, and we cannot ask her to do it again."

"But we can take the money out of team funds," protested Mary Cat.

I was so hungry my sides hurt. I could already feel my teeth sinking into the soft bun, my tongue scooping up the melted cheese. That's why I've been having these funny, dizzy thoughts, I decided. Hunger.

"We've used up the team funds," said Missile.

"That's impossible," I said. "We had that bake sale just last month. We must have money left."

I hate bake sales. I was in charge of the last one. I could have sailed alone to New Zealand, or organized an expedition down the Nile, in the time it took me to run that bake sale. The worst part is bagging the stuff. Tucking sticky brownies into wax paper squares. Dropping handfuls of popcorn into baggies and tying them with twisties. Setting up the tables, posting the signs, making the announcements on the loudspeaker. Bringing enough change.

"We raised forty dollars on that bake sale," said Missile. "That lasted two weeks."

Forty dollars, I thought. I killed a whole month for forty dollars.

Mrs. Fargo turned into the Burger King parking lot. The other half of the team was going to get something to eat whether we drove on or not.

"Oh, Missile, please?" begged Chrissie. "We can pay Mrs. Fargo back. I have enough money on me to pay for two of us, so that's not a whole lot for her to lend us."

Missile sighed.

It was a deep, shaky sigh and it caught at me, like a torn fingernail on stockings. We had just had a winning game. We were going to be second ranked in Region S. Missile should be proud, full of happy laughter. Instead she was tight and tense. "Oh, all right," she said irritably. She swung a U-ie and drove back. The other girls were waiting outside, and when we arrived they did a cheer, complete with high kicks and twirls, although we are anticheerleader and shun anybody who dreams of being a pom-pon girl. Susannah did a one-handed cartwheel right through a puddle and her mother just laughed. Mrs. Fargo is tremendous fun. She cracks jokes nonstop and when you ride with Mrs. Fargo, you laugh so hard you have to beg for bathroom stops or you won't last through another joke.

I felt singularly unlike laughing. We piled out of Missile's car. I rolled up the windows to where they were cracked for a quarter inch of fresh air and locked the doors. "Missile?" I said. My mind was working slowly, like an engine in winter, having a hard time turning over.

"Yes, Tory?"

"How come the boys get the athletic bus and we have to car-pool?"

She took a breath. "For the same reason that the boys get their uniforms laundered free and you have to take yours home to do. Boys count. Girls don't."

I stood there in the rain. It pelted down. Big, fat drops that splattered so hard on my face and into my hair it felt like hail.

Missile's angry features softened and she took my arm like a friend. "Come on, Tory. No point getting upset."

"But it isn't fair," I said.

"True. But there's nothing we can do, so let's go enjoy our hamburgers."

"How come there isn't anything we can do?" I said.

Missile's whole face went tight again. She looked as if she might snap. "Because nobody cares. You think I haven't tried to change things? It can't be done. Now, don't bring it up again, Tory. It makes me so mad I'm afraid I'll —" She broke off and took a very deep breath. I found myself matching it, filling my lungs to loosen my diaphragm and end the stress. We do it before every game. "Just drop it, Tory," said Missile, suddenly weary, as if we had been fruitlessly arguing for hours. She walked without me into the Burger King.

I was the last person in. "Tory!" called Ferris, who was sitting alone at a booth in the corner. "I already got yours. Come sit here."

I shook my head like a puppy and water sprayed around. Missile's right, I thought. No reason to get myself upset over a dumb load of laundry. I trotted over to Ferris. It's nice having a friend who knows you so well she can order your meal for you. Double cheese. Small fries. Vanilla shake. Extra salt and no ketchup. "What a woman," I told Ferris gratefully.

Ferris pulled me down on her side of the booth. "I'm going insane, you know."

"Now, Ferris. You're fine. And you're going to go on being fine. Besides, this is just temporary. In another year and a half you'll be in college and it won't matter where either of your parents lives, or who they remarry."

"But my whole family will be over with!"

"Nobody's whole family is over with, Ferris. Not unless you all crash in the same plane. Now, eat your food while it's hot."

Ferris ate one French fry nibble by nibble, dipping the bitten end into a little puddle of ketchup. "Look intimate," she said to me. "Iowa is coming over. If I hear one more word about the great state of Iowa and the wonderful condition of its athletic departments, I'm going to split her from seam to seam."

"What kind of talk is that from a pacifist?" I said.

Sure enough, Peggy came right over to us. Ferris made a show of looking out the window at the exciting scenery. Which was the cement-block wall of the gas station. Peggy halted, looking miserably around the Burger King for a place where she wouldn't be imposing, but wouldn't feel totally alone either. I felt as sad for her as I do for the dead robin by the side of the road, or the little kid in the grocery whose mother smacks him when he asks for cookies. "Peggy, come on over here. We've got lots of room."

Ferris kicked me under the table and I kicked her back. I'm only five eight, but I have very long legs. Sometimes they come in handy. The one time our team ever got really good newspaper coverage I was described as "lanky." I suppose I have to agree. More bones than flesh, more length than curves.

"Thank you," said Peggy shyly. "I — I thought you might be talking privately, or something, the way you had your heads together."

I shook my head, smiling, to compensate for the face Ferris made, and Peggy slid into the opposite side of the booth. For a while we just ate. Ferris and Peggy ate their fries the same way — like vertical corn on the cob, quarter inch by quarter inch. I just picked up a few and crammed them in. Peggy used a lot of ketchup. I personally loathe ketchup.

"In Iowa," said Ferris suddenly, "do parents get divorced and then remarry and then everybody moves away and leaves you stranded?"

Oh, Ferris, I am so sick of this, I thought. You are being an hysteric. But I didn't let my thoughts show. Ferris is my best friend.

Peggy began flattening her straw. She seemed intent on making it as flat as possible. When she finally had it flattened, she folded it until the straw was completely dead and broken. "In Iowa," she said, "lives a man who is my father except that he got bored being married so he quit. And *here, in this town,* is where my mother grew up and she wanted to come and be near familiar things." Peggy made it sound as if her mother had brought her to a nuclear war zone, complete with fallout and starvation.

For one awful moment I thought Ferris and Peggy would both burst into tears. And then they laughed. Threw back their heads and laughed in unison. "*My* father," said Ferris, happily, and she launched into a really grim tale of what her father had done to them once. "Well, my *mother*," said Peggy, countering with a hideous story of what her mother had done. They burst into gales of laughter at these ghastly stories and put out their palms to smack each other with delight.

"Oh, Tory, isn't that funny?" gasped Ferris, wiping her eyes.

I thought it was appalling, but I said, "Whatever turns you on."

Ferris and Peggy exchanged another round.

I had never actually witnessed a friendship forming. It was sort of like seeing a flower open, or the sun rise. I felt like an environmentalist. Too bad I had no film to capture the moment.

I had a sudden feeling about Kenny. A traitor's emotion. That Kenny and I could never blossom the way Ferris and Peggy were. We could associate, but we couldn't be close.

I slammed the door on that thought.

On one level I still had the feeling, but I wasn't letting it up to where I would actually think it. You know how you can do that, with a thought you absolutely can't tolerate having.

Susannah Fargo appeared just then at the table with a long sheet of yellow lined paper. I recognized the paper. It was torn off Missile's note pad. She uses a legal-sized pad with a spiral binder and takes notes during the games. She might be jotting down that we need to practice weaving. Or she might be remembering that she's out of coffee.

"Bake sale time!" said Susannah gaily.

She extended a pen. It was a blue felt-tipped pen, the kind that writes very narrowly and very beautifully for about one day and then runs out of felt and ink. "Now! Mary Cat has agreed to be in charge this time!" said Susannah, with as much enthusiasm as if Mary Cat had just rescued her first victim in a Red Cross swim. "And! Chrissie and I are going to do popcorn bags and granola sacks. So! Who wants to do brownies? I've also got a slot for peanut-butter cookies. They went really well last time."

All of a sudden I was mad.

Incredibly, painfully mad.

I could not remember being possessed by rage before. It was as if the anger owned me, instead of being just a little piece of emotion I was temporarily displaying.

My Kenny training was deserting me. To be calm like him I'd need major surgery. Our three dates were more like a bandage.

My whole body began to shake. A flush spread over me. I was so mad I was actually burning. "No!" I yelled. "No! No! No! *I won't do it!*"

The whole restaurant turned around to stare. My "No!" vibrated in a suddenly silent room. Susannah stood frozen. Ferris and Peggy sat with matching ketchup-dunked French fries halfway to their mouths. Missile was half out of her seat with shock.

"I'm *sick* and *tired* of this 'Here's a penny, there's a penny' fund raising," I said. "The *boys* don't have to do this! Why should *we*?"

T*wo*

I never have trouble sleeping. I just see a mattress and I start yawning. I love my own bed. It's very old: too narrow for a regular twin mattress, and fitted twin sheets don't work. I have to make hospital corners with flat sheets. It makes me think of old army movies, bouncing a quarter on the sheet after you've pulled it taut.

I cannot remember a night in all my sixteen years when I've gotten onto that mattress, beneath my own sheets and blankets, and not fallen asleep instantly.

Blood raced through me as if it had somewhere special to go. Not just my heart — it could go there any old time. But someplace new, different. Someplace where the blood really had to *run.*

I thought if you had insomnia you would just turn on your light and read for a while and then fall asleep. I hadn't known anxiety would be a physical thing, so that you twitched on the bed, trying the left side, the fetal position, stretching out with your feet hanging off the end. And nothing working. Just the bed creaking, and the floor protesting, and your eyes still wide open, your heart still leaping around like a caged creature.

I kept smoothing my hair back on the pillow, as if to be sure it was really me lying there. My hair is the only thing about me I would never change. It's medium length, thick, dark brown, perfectly cut. It wings back just where I want it to, never falls in my face, looks good when I'm sweaty after a game and when I get out of the shower and when I haven't washed it in five days.

The first time Kenny had ever touched my hair, after our first date, he watched his fingers twine through the locks of silky brown. I waited for him to look back into my eyes, and when he did we kissed and it was marvelous.

Ferris, who is blonde, has very thin hair. During a game it gets soaked and clings to her, coating her skull and neck. Ferris never looks at herself in a mirror until she's had a shower and blown her hair dry. But she doesn't look as bad as Mary Cat. Mary Cat's hair never grows or takes a curl. She braids it to keep it out of her eyes, but the braids don't stay in and by the fourth quarter it's all out. We tell her not to worry — she's so elegant she would look terrific bald — but she worries anyway.

I smoothed my hair and pretended it was Kenny comforting me, but it did no good. Kenny didn't know me well enough yet to offer comfort; he didn't even know what troubled me, let alone how to help with it. Instead, all I could remember was Missile trying to smooth over my tantrum. Trying to iron it away, like an annoying wrinkle.

"Tory," she hissed, "this is neither the time nor the place."

Every single patron of the Burger King stared at me, with wide, greedy, amused eyes, as if I were a spectacle that had come free, like a mug or a Frisbee.

"So the boys get a bus," said Chrissie. "So you have to scream in public about this?"

Ferris said she had enough troubles of her own. She didn't want to take on the world and everybody knew the world wasn't fair.

Peggy said she agreed with Ferris.

Mary Cat said, "I know, Tory, I know. But please, just relax. We just won a big game. Eat a French fry and enjoy. This is not the time to start things."

And then I was crying.

They shoved me back into the booth and sat around me as if it was a huddle during a time-out, giving instructions. Only the instructions were all: "Tory, shut up." "Tory, calm down." "Tory, get a grip on yourself."

I remembered that hateful girl saying I was a St. Bernard puppy. All paws and tongue. I wished Kenny could have been there to be on my side, and then I realized that of all things Kenny would hate a scene.

Finally, Missile just drove me home.

"Missile," I said, speaking over the lump in my throat that had come from crying at the Burger King, "why *do* we have bake sales?"

"Oh, Tory!" she said, and she was half crying herself, snagging herself on tiny shallow breaths that hurt. "I agree with you that it's unfair. I agree we don't want to sell peanut-butter cookies when the boys get it out of the regular school budget, but Tory, I have enough problems."

"Like what?" I said, sulking.

"Like getting better scheduling for our games. We had nearly fifty people come to watch us for an away game. Those people had to drive nineteen miles, Tory, on a week night, to watch you girls play. Because you're good. You're worth it. It was an exciting game. But think how many would have come if it hadn't been the same night as an important boys' game? If it had been scheduled at eight o'clock instead of five-thirty when everybody is still driving home from work? If we gave out school calendars at the beginning of the year that list all the girls' games along with all the boys'? Tory, I can't get into bake sales, don't you understand? That's nothing."

Missile took the corner too sharply and on the wet street we hydroplaned. "Sorry," muttered Missile, slowing down. Water sprayed around us, like a wet, leaping envelope. "The important thing is to keep your perspective, Tory. A lot of things in life are unfair and you have to accept that. Otherwise, you'll spend years in misery. So laugh this off, okay?"

"But Missile," I objected, "you're telling me opposite things. You're saying it's so serious you have to spend all your time fighting — and yet not serious enough for me to do anything but laugh."

Missile pulled into my driveway. She parked so that when I opened the door I'd get a shower of water from the hemlock branches, but I didn't ask her to move. It seemed petty, when we were talking about Life and Fairness, to say, "Drive another three feet, will ya, Missile? I don't want water down my back."

"I guess," said Missile slowly, "that when you take things on, you have to laugh as often as you cry. And you have to do things at the right time, Tory. Crying and yelling at the Burger King is not a very constructive thing to do."

For the umpteenth time I rolled over in bed and looked at my digital clock. The little dots between the hours and the minutes popped back and forth at me, like my pulse. It was 1:11 in the morning. I watched until a 2 appeared and then I tried to sleep by putting my head under my pillow.

I have been in team sports since my first Little League team when I was only eight and couldn't hit a ball unless it was sitting on that big rubber tee they use for little kids.

I love team sports. There's something fierce about it, and real, and important, that I don't feel in, say, chemistry or English grammar. In sports you literally run to the goal. You always know what the goal is. You always know if you've won or lost.

From the day you first join Little League to the day you first shake hands with your opponents at an important high school game, they tell you one thing. *Be fair.* That's why you have a ref — so he'll keep it fair. That's why the crowds scream with fury when they don't agree with the ref — because he isn't being fair. That's why you have rules and fouls and technicals and white lines and basket heights: to keep it fair.

But what's the point in having a good game, playing it fair, keeping it fair . . . when it's all so *unfair* to start with?

I took the pillow off my face and kicked off all the blankets to see if being chilled would help me sleep.

I wished that Kenny and I were close enough for me to call him up and talk about it. Of course, nobody in the whole *world* is close enough for you to call at one in the morning. I dreamed of a day when Kenny and I shared life so intensely that I wouldn't even have to call. He would just know; he would have come!

My pillow was already damp from tears and now I dampened it some more. You would have thought I was trying to grow something in there. If Missile didn't understand — if Ferris, Mary Cat, Chrissie, and Peggy didn't understand — how could Kenny? I would have to explain too much.

Important things, really deep things, like what you think of God, or whether life is fair — these you can only explain to people who already understand.

At two o'clock my mother knocked on my door. "Tory?" she said. "Are you all right? I've been listening to you thrash around for hours."

My family is very privacy oriented. I cannot imagine my parents coming into my bedroom unless I said it was okay, although I cannot imagine saying no, either. "Come on in, Mom."

Neither Missile nor I had given Mom any details about the evening. I think I felt too old to pour out my troubles to my mother. I couldn't sit in her lap anymore. I had to handle it myself. But maybe you're never too old for your mother to comfort you.

My mother shuffled over to my bed. Her bedroom slippers are too large for her. I gave them to her and she refused to exchange them for slippers that fit. She's that way about all my presents. She still wears this gruesome purple blob of a pin I made for her in first grade. It was supposed to be shaped like a pansy, but the leaves didn't stick when the clay went into the kiln and the colors went wrong. I can still remember how excited

I was when she pinned it to her bathrobe Christmas morning and how she wore it to work the very next day.

"Still upset?" She perched on the bed and began running her fingers through my hair. It feels wonderful when someone else does it.

"A little." It felt so good to have her there. My mother is not crazy about my love for sports. The fact that she doesn't like sweat is a big problem, and it upsets her to see my face when I'm really tense because she says it looks as if wires are pulling my cheeks out of line, making me snarl, and she doesn't think pretty girls should do that. She likes basketball only when I dribble neatly around the court and stand quietly and shoot a gentle basket.

Since I never do that, she doesn't go to see me when she has an excuse. Away games are always an excuse.

But still, the thing with my mother is, she loves me. She wears my floppy slippers and my repulsive pin and she reads all my school papers and never runs out of the only breakfast cereal I can stand at six-thirty in the morning.

I started telling her about the bake sale thing. It wasn't easy, because she sort of likes bake sales. She has actually taken time from her own schedule (she's a secretary from eight till five) to make three dozen macaroons for me to sell. She listened to my story in silence, her fingers kneading my back. It's wounderful having a resident masseuse, I thought, and I told her about the boys, and the laundry, and stuff.

"Tory," she said in an appalled voice, "you mean you raised a fuss over having to bake brownies?"

"Yes, Mom. It was kind of a breaking point. I really felt as if I *broke*. As if I used to have a bone somewhere, but it *snapped*, and —"

"Oh, Tory!" said my mother. "I can't imagine you showing such a lack of control. What possessed you?"

"It wasn't fair, Mom. I just didn't see it till that minute. How the boys get —"

"Let's not blame this on the boys. You got overtired in the course of this game and you simply lost control of your manners."

"Mom! It wasn't my manners. It was —"

"You have just as much opportunity as the boys."

"That may be. But do I have just as much money? Do I have just as much time, and gymnasium space, and equipment?"

"Oh, Tory, where's your sense of humor? What does all this stuff matter? You need some sleep, that's all. You'll feel better in the morning. Now, I'll bake the brownies for you, if it's all that agonizing. Although I think it's lacking in team spirit for you to desert your friends like that. The least you can do is bake your own share. In fact, you should make *more* than your share, if you're so worried about team funds."

She had completely missed the point. I

rolled over and looked at her, and it seemed to me that my mother and I were strangers. Could she really have borne me for nine months and brought me up and sheltered me all these years?

"And Tory," said my mother uneasily, "*please* don't make any more scenes. I can't bear the thought of you making a fool of yourself in public. Or — or getting into trouble or something. I can see you flying off the handle, when you're all geared up about unfairness. Marching around. Accusing perfectly innocent people of things. Getting involved with rallies or something. Nice girls don't do that sort of thing."

She was trembling. Her hand shivered in her lap.

My head ached as if I had run skull first into the gym wall.

I guess she took my silence for agreement. "Good," she said briskly. "Well, that's settled then. Good-night, darling."

The tears burned me, like acid, without spilling over. "Good-night, Mom."

The door closed gently behind her. Name one good thing about this night, I screamed silently at the dark.

At three o'clock I was still awake.

Three

By noon the next day, I was known over the entire high school as Tory "No Bake" Travis.

It was awful.

"Here she comes!" someone would cry. "Miss You'll-Never-Get-a-Brownie-Out-of-Me!"

All morning long, people's elbows nudged my ribs, while their wisecracks reddened my face. Never dream for fame and attention. You might get it.

I must have explained my feelings to at least fifty people. "See, the boys get a free bus," I would say earnestly, "while we have to beg our mothers to car-pool. Except that all but two of our mothers work, so those two always have to drive, and pay for their own gas, and that means . . ."

Nobody listened. They were too busy saying things like, "Hey, No Bake! What's cooking?"

Laugh, laugh, laugh. Up and down every corridor in Lockridge High.

"Really, Tory," said Julie, a cheerleader with a habit of sniffing disdainfully at non-cheerleaders. "Right in front of everybody in the entire Burger King! Having a fit! Couldn't you have considered our school's reputation before you disintegrated like that?"

You'd better be careful, I thought, or the hand that holds the pom-pon wil be missing some of its fingers. "It was just the Burger King, Julie," I said irritably. "Not the White House."

"Well, well, well," said Jason Eames. "If it isn't Miss Brownie Points, U.S.A."

I have never liked Jason and now I never will. I considered removing the smile from his face with cleats, but I did not need another scene. Particularly in the hall in front of the principal's office. My mother's fears were still rather loud in my ears.

Our principal is not known for getting involved with mere students, anyhow. When he does, it's usually fatal for the kid. I was probably lucky Dr. Chafee hadn't called me in to a lecture on School Loyalty and United We Stand.

"You know it's a slow season when the only thing the whole school can talk about is Tory's temper tantrum at the Burger King," said Chrissie.

We were all sitting at lunch together, so

that their presence deflected some of the laughter from me.

"That's not fair," said Mary Cat. "It wasn't a temper tantrum, it was a perfectly logical response to an unfair situation. I don't blame Tory a bit."

"Good," I said. "Then we'll boycott having a bake sale."

They gaped at me.

"Tory," said Ferris, laughing but irritable. "That's ridiculous. How can we boycott our own bake sale? You can only boycott other people's bake sales. If we didn't have a bake sale, the only thing that would happen is we'd be even more broke than we are now." She tapped her hard-boiled egg, peeled it neatly, and salted it.

I had the same sinking feeling about Ferris I'd had about my mother. We were strangers. Ferris, wearing the flannel shirt she loves because it makes her feel like a woodsman, although Ferris is a very urban sort. The teeth that were perfect after five years of straightening; all the meals she had missed when her mouth had hurt too much to eat; all the nights we spent at each other's houses; all the giggles and phone calls and —

And I don't know Ferris very well, I thought.

Or she doesn't know me.

Or then again, maybe all I have to do is explain. "Look," I said. "What I think is —"

"Tory, shut up!" said Mary Cat, laughing. "We all know by now what you think." She put her arm around me, but it was her warning arm, the arm she uses on the court when we're getting mad and if we foul again we'll be benched. It was her arm to make me behave.

"Anyhow," said Peggy, sparkling with pleasure, "I know a better way to raise money than bake sales."

"Terrific," said Mary Cat. "What?"

"Let's have a lecture series."

Chrissie nearly spilled her thermos. "It's bad enough that Tory loses her mind in public, Peggy, but we count on our Iowa contingent to do better by us than that."

"No, really. A mock lecture series. For laughs. We'll sell tickets to topics like: Remedial Reading: Beyond the Thrills and Glamour. Or — Gym Lockers: Repositories for Good or Evil?"

Ferris burst into gales of laughter and she and Peggy punched each other lightly. They're not strangers, I thought, tasting loss. They're friends. They understand each other.

"Nope," said Chrissie, "absolutely not. We stick with bake sales. We have a sensation going here now, you know. Tory has given this bake sale publicity like we'd never get otherwise. We could even sell invisible brownies, baked by that famous noncook, Tory Travis."

"Oh, I love it!" cried Mary Cat. "What a scheme! What do you think we could charge for Our Famous Invisible Brownies, Chrissie?"

"But Chrissie!" I said desperately. "Mary

Cat! It's not a joke. I don't want to laugh it off. I lay awake all last night thinking and I want us to take it seriously. I want us to *do* something. As a team."

"About what?" said Chrissie, as if I had not said one single sentence until now. She even looked a little confused. She was not putting me on — she really didn't know what I wanted to do something about.

"I want to make things fair," I said.

There was a startled silence. After a while Ferris said, "Tory, that's all well and good, but we wouldn't even know where to start."

"We could find out."

There was more silence. It wasn't the silence of people thinking hard. It was the silence of people thinking up excuses.

"I don't want to get into stuff like that," said Mary Cat finally. "This is my senior year. I don't want to mess with it. I want to win the championship, get accepted at college, and go to the prom. And that's all."

Ferris finished the last of her egg. "Tory," she said, "it wouldn't accomplish anything except to get us all upset. I have enough problems already. And so does Peggy. Probably all of us. Why, if we took on something like that, God knows where it would lead."

"Anyhow," said Peggy practically, "what would you *do*?"

"I don't know. What did they do back in Iowa, to make things so good?"

Peggy looked blank. "It was always like that."

Chrissie said, "Personally, I think you should bake your share of the brownies and forget about it." Chrissie — who wanted to be the world's most acid-tongued sports commentator? Chrissie believed in baking brownies and forgetting about it?

I had that confused, frustrated energy you get in a game when you're boxed in and nobody on your team opens it up for you and you know you're going to lose the ball.

Mary Cat said, "I am the captain, remember, Tory. And I didn't just abandon you there at the Burger King. I telephoned Missile when we got home and I talked with her for a long time. Missile has tried to fight our athletic department since she got here. Three years now. And she's hardly accomplished a thing. So what can *you* do?"

"If I think of something, would you do it with me?" I said.

There was another long silence. "I doubt it," said Mary Cat at last. "I'm not doing anything to wreck my senior year."

I looked at each of them, and each girl shook her head. Even Ferris. "Just drop it," said Ferris. "You could get burned."

They had all finished eating. I'd been talking so much I hadn't even started. One by one they left. Like a team — touching me. *Chin up. Good move. Hang in there, kid.*

But they weren't going to play the game.

I was the only person at a six-seat table. At the beginning of lunch period it would mean serious unpopularity — now, with everyone straggling out, it meant nothing. I chewed a tasteless bread crust. If the sandwich had had a filling, I hadn't noticed it.

And then Kenny slid into the seat next to me. He doesn't have my lunch period. He could only have come by cutting class. I was equally worried and flattered. "Hi," he said softly. I love Kenny's voice. It is low and melodic. I think he should be a television anchorman. His voice is authoritative, but friendly and warm. If he announced hurricane warnings, you would think it was nothing, only a drizzle, probably rather pleasant in its way.

I took his hand instantly and squeezed it, thinking, I do have an ally. I have Kenny. I felt this funny shifting, like a sky going from gloom to rainbow. His hand was larger than mine but it felt no stronger. It just felt solid.

"Tory," he said. Not his usual voice. There was uncertainty in it.

"What?" I said. I looked past his eyes to his floppy hair and thought, He cut class to talk to me.

"What's this weird story I'm hearing?" The rainbow shattered like glass.

Weird. Kenny Magnussen would never associate with a girl who was weird. It made me so anxious I thought my hair would turn gray. I could lose him, I thought. "I was tired. My nerves got frayed in the game, Kenny."

"Then it really happened? You really blew up at the Burger King? Tory. God."

He wasn't confusing me and God. He was giving me my mother's whole lecture in a three-letter word. He was saying, *How* could *you make a scene?*

I abandoned any idea of trying to explain what I had understood out there in the rain, about boys and girls and fairness and the lack of it. Bad enough I'm halfway to being a jock, I thought. Bad enough to be angular instead of curvy. I've got a terrific boy almost by the hand. I can't act weird and lose him. I said, "It won't happen again."

He smiled at me. "Good." It was firm, like the evening wrap-up. "I think it's being on the team, Tory. It wears you out too much. I hope you don't take up another sport next season. You should have more free time."

My heart soared. He wasn't writing me off — he was implying that the free time I would have come spring would be ours to share.

Kenny touched my sleeves with his fingertips. There was hardly enough pressure to feel him there. He ran his fingers very lightly down my arms, and then up again, and into my hair. I felt as if my soul were shivering. "Our hair is the same color, did you know that?" he said.

"Yes. I knew that." If he had asked me to elope with him, I would have done it on the spot.

"I gotta run," he said softly. He touched the corner of his mouth with his tongue, and watching that was like being kissed, only his face was still a foot away. "See you this afternoon?" he said. "I've got the car."

"Wonderful," I said, and it was. Full of wonder, wonder-full. Kenny and me. I had almost thrown it away again, as stupidly as I had that day in seventh grade.

Kenny walked out of the cafeteria. I stared into my dried-out sandwich and thought, I have absolutely got to behave. Nothing matters more than being the kind of girl Kenny wants.

If there had been a full-length mirror in the cafeteria, I would have stood in front of it and studied myself. *So this is the girl Kenny Magnussen likes,* I would think, checkout every inch, wondering how it could be. Looking at the hair (which *was* perfect) and at the rest of the body (which was not) and thinking — How do I stay just right? How do I stay away from weird?

Keep Kenny.

K.K. I could put it on my papers, write it on the corners of my calendar, and paint it with nail polish in the trim of my makeup mirror at home. Nobody would know what it meant. Keep Kenny.

But the world does not wait for you to keep Kenny, or anything else, for that matter. Other people are all out there, muddying the water, jumping in where you thought there was silence, interfering where you thought everything was neatly arranged.

Dusty, Aaron, and Mike of the boys' basketball team sat down with me. Now

Dusty is okay, though a turkey. Aaron and Mike are different. The word "wholesome" definitely does not apply to them. They're the kind of kids that make you feel like staying home and playing Monopoly by yourself.

Aaron sat on my left. Dusty on my right. Mike across from me. I could feel trouble like a rash. "Hi, guys," I said. I folded my napkin twice and stopped, because it made me look nervous. I *was* nervous, but it was poor tactics to look that way. I wished fervently that Kenny had stayed.

"Couldn't help overhearing your little chat with your girl friends," said Aaron.

"Cute idea," said Mike. "Doing something about the terrible discrimination you tykes suffer. But you seem to be all alone, Tory honey." He made a big show of looking around for a team, peering around empty chairs.

"Hey," said Dusty, as though this wasn't what he expected them to say. "Hey, Mike."

Mike ignored Dusty. "How you going to make things fair, Tory?" he said. "You going to rip off the boys?"

"Why should you be ripped off just because we are?" I said. "I'd like to see things even. Fair. The same all around." Thoughts of keeping Kenny dissolved in my anger.

Mike and Aaron exchanged amused looks. They had a plan and whatever it was, I would have preferred to be in chemistry. But if I got up now, I would be running away and I refused to give them the satisfaction.

"You're all talk," said Aaron. He grinned, all his teeth exposed as if he wanted me to floss them. "If life is so unfair, you ought to be out there doing something about it, Tory, instead of just whining in the cafeteria corner. Show us the stuff you liberated girls are made of."

Do something, indeed. My teammates had just established that nobody knew what to do, my boyfriend had made it clear he didn't want me doing anything, anyway. I sat matching Aaron's smirk with a little pretend boredom. I wasn't bored at all. I was furious and scared. Watch it, Tory, I thought, don't make another scene. Keep Kenny.

Dusty said rather lamely, trying to be courteous about it, "We were just curious about what you thought you could really do, Tory. Boycotts? I don't really get it."

"I haven't worked it out yet," I said.

Mike and Aaron laughed and my insides shriveled. "Let me give you a little guidance," said Mike. Dusty looked uncomfortable. "In a high school, generally speaking, the principal is in charge. So why don't you have a little chat with our principal about all this dreadful unfairness?" He said *dreadful* in a vicious, stabbing way, mimicking me and all girls.

"Thanks, Mike. When a fellow has only one good idea every decade, a girl should be gracious enough to use it. I will definitely have a little chat with our principal." I opened my brown bag and carefully put my garbage in it. Chrissie had left a bit of apple and Ferris had forgotten some of her eggshell. I scooped that up in a napkin and threw it away, too. It kept me busy.

"Nice little housekeeper, isn't she?" said Mike to Aaron.

"Comes naturally to girls," said Mike.

"Tory," said Dusty in an apologetic voice to me.

"Now would be the perfect time to go see Dr. Chafee," said Aaron. "Tell you what, Tory. Since your own team won't support you, Mike and Dusty and I will go along. Give you a little confidence."

The rage I had suffered yesterday was back. My insides churned and bubbled. "I have a class," I said.

"So Dr. Chafee will give you a late pass," said Aaron. "Listen, Tory. We heard your pep talk. This stuff is important. You shouldn't let it go another minute."

I stood up. "Excuse me. I have to get to class."

Aaron didn't move out of my way. "What's the matter, Tory? You scared?"

"Most girls are scared of doing anything," said Mike. "Look how her friends scurried off the moment she suggested action. Girls aren't up to it. Besides, Tory doesn't have Kenny's permission."

I was choking on my own fury. But I said as calmly as I could, "I am certainly not scared. And I don't need anybody's permission. I'll make an appointment with Chafee."

"She's scared," said Mike to Aaron. "She's trying to go formal and school-teachery on us, but she's scared."

I am not the type who confronts principals. I am the type who avoids them. Dr. Chafee has never been seen at a single girls' sporting event. Not one field hockey game, not one softball game, not one gymnastic meet, not one basketball game. Naturally he's busy, what with going to all the boys' games. He did agree to shake hands with the captain of last year's girls' team — but just for the photograph for the newspaper when they won the championship.

It made me even more furious just thinking about Chafee.

"Hey, gang!" yelled Aaron. It was a huge yell, borne of years on courts and playing fields. A yell that carried. "Tory's going to talk to the principal! Come on, everybody! Let's get in on this."

"Jeez, Aaron, that's not fair," said Dusty, "Tory didn't even say she —"

But it was too late.

The whole cafeteria began yelling and laughing. Chairs banged and scraped. The soft, papery squash of garbage being hurled into cans filled the room. "Way to go, Tory!" yelled a bunch of sophomore girls.

"Another scene?" somebody remarked.

Scene. This time right in school.

"I'm coming along!" a boy yelled. "Just let me do my last trig problem."

My heart stopped, fluttered, and started

up again. Faster. Aaron laughed. I could have drilled his teeth with a jackhammer. The bum leaned over and patted my hair.

"Hurry up, Tory, the next class is only seven minutes away," said some girl. "Take the west stairs, it's quicker. What are you going to say?"

Oh, my God, I thought. *How did I get into this?* Two days ago I was an ordinary high school kid daydreaming about cutting chemistry and forgetting to do my French.

Now —

Oh, God.

Talk to Chafee? About *what*? All I had were some cloudy ideas of things not being fair, some complaints about bake sales, some feelings that things should be different.

I have to plan a speech, I thought. Write things down. Look things up. Talk to Missile first. Think about this.

They weren't giving me time to think. I was like a seashell at high tide, swept up with the seaweed and dropped on the sand whether I wanted it or not.

If I fail, they'll laugh, I thought. And not just at me. At the team. At girls.

At least thirty people were charging up the stairs with me. There would have been more, except it was the tail end of lunch.

Dear God, let Chafee be out of town.

"Not scared, are you, Tory?" said Mike, in a falsely loving voice.

"Of course not." I felt like flu. My bones ached and my throat was sore and I felt the loss of sleep last night like a missing finger.

Okay, you're going to have to do this. Calm down. Plan. Chafee is just a person. Think of him combing his bald spot. Don't panic. Panic before a game and you can't play.

There was no way to stop it. I had no way out.

And then I saw Peggy. I sagged. Peggy could prove beyond a shadow of doubt that in Iowa, they didn't do this sort of thing. And having honed her speech on the team so often, think what a polished talk she could deliver to Chafee. "Peggy! Let's —"

"Oh, Tory," said Peggy, backing up. "I understand. I really do. But —"

"But!" I cried. "What do you mean — *but*?"

Peggy flushed scarlet. Right in front of Aaron and Mike she said — mumbled, "My mother wouldn't like it."

Aaron and Mike howled with laughter. Peggy fled. I thought, *Her* mother wouldn't like it. Oh, God, what about my mother?

But it was not a reason I could use in front of Aaron and Mike. Never.

There was no one around me I knew well. No one to go in with me. Just miscellaneous, assorted kids, going along for the ride.

The boys herded me into the secretaries' domain and the bunch of us filled the little waiting area. The clerk looked genuinely alarmed, as if she figured we were the beginnings of a violent student riot. Don't worry, I thought. I'm the only one on my team.

Oh, Kenny. I thought. Please give me a third chance. I couldn't get out of this. I really couldn't.

Dusty opened the door for me — the door that read: PLEASE KNOCK FIRST.

And in the space of that door opening I had another thought fall into place, as if the winter engine had been grinding away down there, and gears were meshing when I didn't even know it.

Last night, lying awake, I'd thought of how, if a referee wasn't fair, people got mad at him. At *him*. That was the pronoun. Even the people who run the girls' games are men, I thought. We've never had a woman referee. And someone had told me once (although at the time I hadn't listened) that we get worse refs, because they don't pay as much to ref a girls' game as they pay to ref a boys' game.

Kenny, I can explain, I thought. Really and truly, there are things that aren't fair. I'll explain in the car this afternoon.

The door finished its swing to reveal Dr. Chafee.

Looking up with a frown, he was ready to reprimand the person trespassing on him. His eyes barely focused on me, but went immediately to Dusty, Mike, and Aaron. Dusty ushered me in, shutting the door quietly behind me, and Dr. Chafee looked at me with three expressions that crossed his face in quick succession: Surprise — the girl had come in. Relief — only the girl had come in. And amusement — the girl had come in.

F_our_

"I am Victoria Travis," I told him. If he had ever been to a girls' basketball or softball game he would have known, but of course he hadn't.

He didn't yell at me. He didn't mention any pressing appointments. And he knew, and I knew, that it was because of the boys in the waiting room, not because of the girl in front of him. "Well, Victoria," he said — raising a nicely matched pair of eyebrows over a face dark with winter vacation tan — and smiled above his preppy clothing. "What may I do for you? I gather you are the spokesman for that little group?" He laughed gently and apologized. "Perhaps I mean spokes-*person.*"

Stupid word, I thought, launching into my talk without any preliminaries. I skipped the weather forecast and went straight into the sports report.

"I want to talk about our athletic department," I said. "I want to point out some of the unfairness that we're running into, in case you aren't aware of it."

First I talked about the things that took money — like uniforms, laundry, and buses. Then I talked about the things that didn't — like game times. Then about how we had to do our own fund raising — the bake sales.

In basketball when you do a good job, it's obvious. You score or you don't. You win or you don't. But it's hard to tell with words; they come out of your mouth but they go into somebody else's ears. Who knows if they hear what you meant to say?

But one thing I knew. Without preparation, without an assignment, without even knowing how, I had said the right things in the right order. I felt pride like something solid. The knots in my stomach were gone. I was in control.

This is how I'll explain it to Kenny, I thought. Calm and organized. Like the evening news. Kenny can respond to that.

I think I actually expected Chafee to shake my hand. To jump up, crying, "Thank goodness you told me, Tory. I'll correct it right away!"

What he did was rock (creak, really, in his comfortable leather swivel chair) with this glazed look on his face. The look kids get in English when the teacher explains the inner meaning of poems. "Well, Victoria," he said at last. He rearranged some papers and covered them with a shiny, glass unicorn paperweight. "How very informative."

I waited. It's not one of my better skills.

Small, neat frowns came and went on Chafee's face. Finally he said, "I'm proud of my girls, Victoria." He went on about how proud he was of us, and how lovely we were, and what fine, fine futures lay ahead of us.

At first I thought this was his introduction and he would get to things like team funds any moment.

But he didn't. He began tamping a pipe. I waited for him to light it and then talk, but he lit it and puffed. Quietly, meditatively.

I had done something wrong. I had blown it. He was just bored, waiting for me to wrap up and leave him alone. I looked down at my hands. They were trembling like my mother's last night.

What was my mother going to say about this?

I should leave, I thought. Nobody will know what happened in here. I should give up before I get into trouble and my mother finds out. But what my mouth said was, "I was hoping something could be done about it. Changes."

Dr. Chafee merely looked at me through a cloud of smoke and smiled pityingly.

Right up until that moment I never understood what took people so long to fight injustice. How come they just stood there, letting it happen to them? Now I knew. It was because you have to beg. Someone sits there creaking his comfortable chair, sucking on his pipe, looking bored — and you have to beg. *Please, sir, please be interested, please care, sir.*

Begging was worse than anxiety.

But what else could I do? "Changes to — you know — make things fair." I added, hopelessly.

"Victoria, Victoria." He shook his head. "We're not talking about fairness or the lack of it. We're talking here about dollars. Now, no one regrets more than I that the dollar must enter into areas where previously it was never considered. Surely you know the toll that inflation, OPEC, and the new federal administration have taken upon our educational facilities?"

I knew all about it. It was my father's favorite (sometimes his only) topic.

"We must all learn to be thrifty, Victoria," said Dr. Chafee.

"The girls have always been thrifty," I said. "I don't think the dollar ever was considered for us. I think the boys should start being thrifty as well."

Both of his eyebrows shot up. If I had suggested a course in building hand grenades, he could not have been more astounded. Either his fine, fine girls did not argue with him, or boys and thrift were not expected to go together.

Outside the bells rang. I could hear pounding feet, a cluttery racket of hundreds of kids talking and moving. At least if the boys failed to be thrifty, they would have to go on to their next class. They wouldn't be out there waiting for me, their jeers at the ready.

Dr. Chafee then made himself even more comfortable. I couldn't do that. My chair was practically a vertical coffin with slats. He told me about school boards and budgets, about school superintendents and state requirements. About the atmosphere of our times. And most of all about how his girls — his fine, fine girls — needed to be aware of such massive obstacles.

I'm not your girl, I thought. If I were your girl, I'd have seen you at some of the basketball games. "Don't you think," I said carefully, "that in our times, the atmosphere should also be good for the girls?"

"Victoria, the money is allocated for the year and my hands are tied." He actually held his wrists up, to show how they were joined by money already entered in different columns.

Teachers have a special smile they turn on when they're done talking. It isn't a smile at all. It's a facial twitch that means, Go, bolt, leave me in peace, class is over.

Dr. Chafee smiled.

"Then what about next year?" I said.

It was queer. I had never once thought about next year. I knew that next year was going to arrive, and I knew that during it I would be a senior, but I had never really looked in that direction. Junior year was too full. Now I had a vision of a calendar rising like mountains — little valleys of vacation and great snowy ranges of school. Going on for years.

Years when we might as well have money for the girls, too.

"But," said Chafee, and he leaned forward and gave me a wonderful smile. A real smile.

But, I thought excitedly, he's going to make an effort. He does understand. I misjudged him. It was worth it coming in here. He'll probably —

"But I am impressed with your efforts, Victoria. I know how delighted your English teacher will be to know what a fine verbal presentation you gave me. Oral skills, you know, my dear, are very important."

I had actually sat up in my chair to beam at him — like a little girl waiting for a lollipop. I jerked the smile off my face and sat, frozen, humiliated, enraged. His smile stayed on his face, caught like a kite on a telephone wire.

"Have a good week, Victoria," he said, getting up, waving me out of his office. "Now try to keep your perspective. There's no good in getting upset over things that can't be helped, you know."

I had heard that line before. It was beginning to look as though there must be some truth in it, because people said it so often. I stood up, too. He put his hand out to shake mine and it was like after a game, when the losers and the winners have to shake.

"Well," I said, struggling to think how my

mother would handle this situation, "thank you for your time."

"Not at all, Victoria. Feel free to come in anytime you have problems."

The hall contained nothing but silence and the faint smell of disinfectant where the janitor had passed by with his pail. From the corner came the distant, quiet murmur of classes begun without me.

No wonder Peggy had declined!

I felt as if Chafee and I really had played some sort of game. And he had won. By fouling.

I could not just stand there in the hall, exposed. I had to go someplace private and calm down.

I chose the bathroom. At Lockridge the bathrooms are enormous white-tiled places, with white cubicles and white sinks and glass brick to let in the sun. You have to squint to go to the toilet. Today it was empty except for one girl putting a quarter into the tampon machine. I didn't know her. I was lucky. I could have run into half the school cutting class to smoke.

I soaked a paper towel with cold water and pressed it against my eyelids. Chemistry, I thought miserably. I have to go to chemistry.

First I have to throw up.

I shut the door on myself and stood in the little cubicle but I didn't actually get sick. On the other hand, I didn't get better.

Chemistry.

I have the two wimpiest boys in the entire school for my chem lab partners. There's Jonathan, who won't touch anything. Ever. He plays the cello and he's convinced whatever liquid he gets near is a corrosive acid and might remove his fingertips. So *he's* useless. And there's Andy, who has never listened to a teacher in his entire life, which can be a real problem in chem lab. He's also too dumb to read, so written directions don't help. He has a habit of splashing madly, adding whatever seems to be on hand in whatever proportion turns him on, and he likes to cook this over a Bunsen burner he doesn't even light until the entire lab is filled with gas.

Right now I could not even think about Jonathan and Andy, let alone work with them. I checked the late pass. Good. It was neither dated nor timed. I'd skip the whole lab and sit it out in the girls' room. The toilet cubicle was giving me claustrophobia. I went out and wet the paper towel with more cold water. My forehead was so hot the towel had gotten warm. The tiles on the wall were chilly. I leaned on them to let the cold relax the veins in my forehead.

Forget it, I said to myself. Stop worrying about it. So things are rough. So you made a fool of yourself. So the entire school will know because Aaron and Mike will make sure of it. So your mother will go berserk. Small stuff. Relax. Forget it.

Think about Kenny instead. Keep Kenny,

remember? Think about how you have just proved to him that you are weird. Launching yourself at Chafee like a rocket doomed to failure. A scene to end all scenes. Just what Kenny wanted in a girl friend. A crazy loudmouth with a cause.

Kenny's car was always parked in the far west side of the parking lot. Not under the tree, because he didn't want any debris falling on it, but off to the side where nobody would open a door against it and dent him. A private corner, actually, where you could survey the school but not be spied on in return.

Well, Kenny would not be there when I went out. He would be long gone, reversing his father's red Corvette or his mother's white Datsun and leaving fast, before Weird Tory could corner him.

I could not understand how my life had collapsed so fast. I hadn't planned a single minute of this. I hadn't even stopped to think about any of it. It had all just happened.

If this is what life's going to be like, I thought morosely, I decline. I quit. I want to put in for more planning time.

"Tory?"

I jumped, knocking myself against a sink and mirror at the same time. We ball players are widely known for our superior coordination. It was the skinny girl I'd forgotten about.

"Oh, I'm sorry," she said. "I didn't mean to startle you. Are you all right?"

"I'm fine," I said, hoping she would interpret this as meaning, I'm rotten and leave me alone.

She couldn't take a hint. She stood there tugging her blouse down under her skirt so it wouldn't bag at the waist. I haven't worn a skirt to school all year. "I'm Beth Martin," she said. "You don't know me."

Don't want to, either, I thought wearily. I need this whole period to pull myself together. Although it is beginning to look as if I'll need the entire weekend.

Or maybe even the year.

"I wanted to tell you how wonderful we think you are," said Beth Martin. She blushed. "Nobody from lunch has talked about anything else. It's just so terrific of you, standing up for what's right instead of being a shriveled-up little scaredy-cat like everybody else. And then to march right into Dr. Chafee's office and let him have it — wow!"

Her voice was reverent. Her eyes shone. "Now that you're getting your basketball team what's fair for it," she went on, "I'm hoping you'll work on field hockey next."

She looked at me the way little kids in department stores look at Santa Claus. I covered my eyes with the wet towel. "We don't even have field hockey this year," I protested. "The field is bumpy. You can hardly walk across it, let alone play."

"That's the point! The field should be treated as carefully as a baseball diamond:

flattened and seeded and all that. Last year they used up all the maintenance money on the football field and when Miss L checked out our field, it was so bad we'd have broken our ankles. *That's* why the sport was dropped."

I was dumbfounded.

"Not to mention," said Beth, mentioning it with rage, "that we're missing half the shin guards and the hockey sticks have splinters."

No wonder I had always disliked that game.

"Lots of girls rejoiced when we didn't have field hockey this year," said Beth, "and that's okay. If they want to sing in the chorus, or paint stage sets, or belong to Dungeons and Dragons Club, that's okay. But *I* want to play field hockey and that should be okay, too."

Basketball was my sport. I participated in the others, but I hardly even noticed them go by until we started softball, which I also loved. I wondered if the field hockey team (last year when we had one) ran bake sales. Car pools. Taped the splinters from their sticks.

"It's because it's a girls' sport," said Beth darkly. "You notice that the boys never run out of money."

"Yes," I said. "I noticed that."

F*ive*

Kenny was there.

He had his father's old red Corvette — the smashing kind that looks about ready to eat its own headlights. He was sitting in the driver's seat and there was no expression on his face at all, even when he glanced at me trudging toward him. He looked like a model for a tobacco ad — distant, removed, masculine, and sexy.

I wanted to gallop around the car, leap in the passenger side, and throw my arms around him, but instead I walked slowly up to the driver's side. His window was rolled down and his elbow was resting on the top, his fingers curled over the roof of the car. It was cold and the wind ruffled his floppy hair.

He said to me, "You coming?"

Well, a lukewarm welcome was better than none. I walked around the car and got in. My insides hurt so much from all the stress of the day I thought my stomach was probably thinner. I sat down hard, trying to think of something affectionate and interesting to say, but I lost my balance going down and dropped my books on the floor where they crushed my feet. What I actually said was, "Ooooh, my toes."

Kenny reached over me and pulled the seat belt around to latch it across my shoulder. His face was within millimeters of mine but it didn't show on *his* face as anything particularly thrilling. He just looked exasperated. He sat back, pulled his own seat belt on, so that we were forever separated, locked into position away from each other, and said, "Tory, I don't believe you." He started the car and we left the parking lot.

"I didn't believe it, either, Kenny. It wasn't what I had in mind. Truly. It just happened."

"Tory, how could something like that just happen? You went and organized the entire *lunchroom* to go up to the principal's office? In like one half of one minute after I left you? *Jeez.*"

"No, Kenny, really, I didn't organize anything. All those people just came along. There would have been more except that most people were still eating or were trying to finish their homework or something."

"How did they know to come along? Did you announce to the whole place that you needed an assault team?"

"No, Mike and Aaron did that."

"*Mike and Aaron?* You are that close to

57

them? That's the trouble with girls being in sports, Tory. You end up hanging around with jerks like Mike and Aaron."

"I don't hang around with them!" I yelled. "I don't even like them. And there's no trouble with girls being in sports."

"Let's not get off on side issues," said Kenny.

"It's not a side issue," I said. "I have to —"

"All I want to know is, is there something between you and Mike and Aaron?" he said.

"Certainly not. Unless you count hostility and hatred. They don't matter in the slightest, Kenny. What matters is *why* it all happened. It's an issue of *fairness*."

"Tory, you've gotten me so tense I can hardly drive," said Kenny. This when he looked so calm you would have thought he was posing for a tranquilizer advertisement. I was the one trying to shred the fabric of my seat belt. "Let's drop it, okay?" said Kenny. "I don't want to argue with you."

Well, I certainly didn't want to argue with Kenny. I wasn't really even sure what we were yelling about. But it definitely wasn't my idea of the perfect date. "Right," I said. Kenny smiled at me. He has wonderful smile control. It seems to me he can turn out smiles the way thermostats can turn out degrees of heat. This smile showed his teeth, and half of one of his two dimples, but it was not a whole smile. I like his totally relaxed smile when his dimples (they are both in the same cheek, and not very deep; just enough to make you want to touch them) tuck in and his eyes crinkle and his whole face lights up under his floppy hair.

"Let's go over to the Y, okay?" suggested Kenny. "I'm really in the mood for exercise and it's raw and drizzly and crummy out and that hot pool would feel great."

"Okay. We'll have to swing by my house to get my suit and towel."

"No problem."

So we drove all the way back across town to my house while Kenny talked about our first date. The movie. It was like a soft blanket covering me. Good things, warm things, things I wanted repeated. And so did Kenny, or he'd never talk like this.

While Kenny waited in the car I ran in to get my bathing suit. I ran my fingers over the material. Kenny had seen me in a swimsuit before, of course, since we were both Y members, but he had probably never really *liked* me when he saw me. Now he liked me. This afternoon was proof positive.

We giggled all the way to the Y. It was the kind of afternoon every girl daydreams about: a terrific boy, laughter, fingers that touch and lips that are going to. We parted company at the front desk and went off to separate dressing rooms to change and I wondered if Kenny was thinking of me at the stage between jeans and bathing suit the way I was thinking of him.

The smell of the pool rose up to meet me. Chlorine, sweat, and used towels in damp, hot air. People's shouts ricocheted like bullets off the pale yellow tiles of the walls and floors. With every leap off the three diving boards came the metallic *whack!* of the board springing back and the magnified splash of a body hitting water. The humidity was suffocating.

I'm not a good swimmer. My rhythm is off and I'm awkward. It used to embarrass me horribly. Now it just embarrasses me a lot.

I sat on the rim letting the emotions of the day drain through my legs into the warm water, and I thought about harmless things like the color of my toenail polish.

People are anonymous at a pool. Oh, sure, you notice the really handsome ones, or the terrific divers, but basically there's just a clutter of swimsuits and bathing caps and wet hair. It's hard even to recognize people because they're so different in bathing trunks than they are in sweaters. The anonymity made me feel safe. No Aaron, no Mike, no Chafee.

But I was not anonymous. Kenny found me instantly. "You look terrific," he said, and his smile was all the way on. Because of me. "Thanks," I said. "So do you."

We giggled. You don't usually tell a boy how good he looks. Especially when you don't mean his clothes because he's hardly wearing any. Kenny looked like a weight lifter in repose. I could not take my eyes off him. At the far end of the pool a girl climbed up a ladder. I thought about climbing up Kenny.

"I have to apologize to you for that day

you asked me out and I was so mean to you."

"You remember that?" said Kenny, astonished. "That was an eternity ago. We must have been twelve or something."

"It was rotten of me, no matter how old we were."

Kenny nodded. "It was pretty bad," he conceded. "The guys reminded me of that every day in the locker room for the next year."

"Oh, Kenny! I'm sorry. How awful."

"Forget it. It made me tough." Kenny demonstrated that his skin was now tough as medieval armor. "Race you to the end of the pool?"

"You're on."

We slipped into the water, splashed each other, grinned through the wet, and headed down the tiles. Kenny beat me easily. When I finally churned in at the end, he was sitting calmly on the pool rim swinging his feet in the water, looking at what I hoped was a waterproof watch.

I vaulted out to sit next to him. (Another thing I did when I was twelve was learn how to get out of a pool. I wanted to look like a mermaid, not a flounder. When other people were practicing their strokes, I was practicing my exit — which may explain why my stroke is so lousy.)

Water trickled down Kenny's back and clung to the hairs on his chest. I felt dizzy just being next to him. This is what being in love is like, I thought. We're not casual anymore. At least, I'm not. This is far more.

Kenny said, "I feel like a movie."

"Funny, you don't look like one," I said.

We both laughed lightly and our faces came together. We touched noses and laughed again and I think we would have kissed each other, right there in front of the whole free swim, but an anxious voice said, "Tory?"

I was so startled I almost slid off the tiles back into the pool. Kenny looked ever so slightly irritated, which, knowing his self-control, meant he was really very irritated. It was a girl named Heidi something or other, a senior I hardly knew. She sat down next to me, ignoring Kenny completely.

"Hi, Heidi," I said, surprised.

"Hello, Heidi," said Kenny courteously. I liked him for that. I liked knowing he would never be rude.

Heidi didn't even answer Kenny, just waved at him. Abruptly she said, "Tory, do you have a moment?"

Her face was tight and nervous, like the moment the SAT exams are actually passed out. "What's wrong, Heidi?" I said, getting nervous just seeing her expression. I could not imagine how I could be in a position to help Heidi with anything, but my mind rattled through possible problems — needing a ride home, a towel, bra repair, change for the phone.

"When are you going back to the principal, Tory?" she said.

"Back?" I repeated, astonished.

"She isn't," said Kenny.

Heidi gave Kenny the sort of look you reserve for annoying little problems and turned back to me. "People are saying you talked only about the problems on the basketball team, Tory. It isn't just basketball. It's everything."

Kenny blew out his breath in a sharp, hard exclamation and his body stiffened. He turned slightly away from both of us.

"Like tennis," said Heidi. "There are two courts, right? And you notice that the boys' court is the southside court and the girls always play on the eastside court?"

I never used the school courts. I learned tennis in the Park-Rec program run by the city in the summer. At school the courts are always full of puddles and the nets sag and the rackets are crummy. But, I reflected, school equipment usually is lousy. That's why we always end up buying our own stuff.

"See," said Heidi, "the south court is high and dry and smooth. Which is why the girls get the east court — where it's cracked and wet and uneven."

"I don't know much about the school tennis program," I said to Heidi. "I have my own racket. The school stuff is too crummy to use."

Kenny said, "I'm going to swim a little." He slid into the water without looking at me or waiting for me to respond.

I wanted to shove Heidi into the pool and go after Kenny, but I couldn't interrupt her.

Whatever she was saying was important to her, and I had had enough lately of not being allowed to say what was important to me.

Under the water Kenny was filmy. The water condensed him and changed his whole structure. He really did look like a butterfly swimming. Kenny surfaced at the far end of the pool, shook his head like a dog, and blinked his eyes to get the water out. I waved, in case he saw me, but he didn't wave back.

Because he didn't see me, I told myself, not because he didn't want to.

The puddle of water around me was getting cool.

"No, Tory," said Heidi. "It isn't the school stuff that's too crummy to use. It's the *girls'* stuff that's too crummy to use."

You would have thought I'd hired a small plane to do some skywriting for me: TORY TRAVIS TAKING IN ATHLETIC DEPARTMENT COMPLAINTS AT THE Y FROM FOUR TO FIVE THIS AFTERNOON. TAKE ADVANTAGE OF THIS UNUSUAL OPPORTUNITY.

"Kenny, don't be mad," I said, going home. "I can't help what happened."

"Of course you can help it. You can say no. You can say, 'Go away.' You can say, 'I'm not interested.'"

He drove with exaggerated caution. If I had my license and if I got angry, I would whip around corners and jump lights. And probably cause accidents, I thought miserably, envying him his calm. How did he get all that calm? How was it that Heidi and the other girls had stirred me up so much my insides felt set adrift — roiling in some private tempest — and yet Kenny could merely raise an eyebrow and express mild irritation?

Kenny said, "I think you're getting hysterical about this. I mean, we're talking tennis rackets here. Hockey sticks. Not nuclear war. It's not something to bring up before the Supreme Court, Tory."

"I didn't say it was!" I cried.

"See. You're yelling about it."

"I'm not yelling!" I yelled. I took a very deep breath. "You're right. I'm yelling. There. I've stopped yelling."

Kenny laughed and took my hand. He drove for two blocks one-handed, not an easy trick with a standard transmission. I bent over and kissed the back of his hand and my hair fell on his arm and he said, "I'm crazy about your hair."

"That's because it's just like yours," I said.

"Yeah, but it's on you." He grinned at me and my heart flipped. How could someone as calm as Kenny be taking me on such an emotional roller coaster?

I forgot about being cautious, and keeping things calm and slow and I said, "Want to come to the basketball game Friday night, Kenny? Afterward we could go somewhere?"

Kenny said, "I thought the game was Thursday."

"That's the boys. We're Friday." I thought,

Kenny's never seen me play. Will he be impressed! On the other hand, if I botch everything up, will I be humiliated. Oh, well, you have to expect these things. The important part is, Kenny and I will go out afterward, and if we've won the game, Kenny and I will celebrate together, and if we've lost, Kenny and I will commiserate.

Kenny said, "I don't know, Tory. I mean, I'm glad you like basketball and all, but I'm not excited about it enough to go to two games in one week, and I'm going to the boys' game the night before."

He was so polite about it. Gentle, as if I were an old lady. You're killing me, I thought. You're saying it sweetly and kindly and it's like pouring acid down my throat. If you really liked me, you'd go to all my games.

But that wasn't fair. I shouldn't force my interests on him. That was the trouble with me lately. Too forceful.

We drove another block, not touching now. I thought, Ask me out on Saturday. Suggest a movie. Suggest anything. Don't let it sit there, please, Kenny.

But he said nothing more. And so when we got to my house I was stiff and awkward and hurt and I could hardly even bear to look at him. Tory, you are not engaged to marry this guy, I lectured myself. You have had a big three dates. Four — if you count this afternoon. He has no weekend obligation to you. It's okay to let the relationship move along slowly.

Except I hate things that move along slowly. I like things that fly.

I picked up my suit and towel, and they had left damp marks on the upholstery. I dabbed at the wetness with my towel, which just made it worse. "Don't worry about it," said Kenny, and he smiled his littlest smile — the one he probably gives to salesmen at the shoe store. "See you around," he added.

See you around.

The awfulest three words in the English language. Of course he'd see me around. We were at the same high school, weren't we? I didn't want to see him around. I wanted to see him at home and at the movies and in the backseat and after school and —

"Right," I said. "Thanks, Kenny. See you."

S^{ix}

I was home before either of my parents.

We have a household rule that the first one home makes supper, the second one home does the cleanup, and the third one home is probably too tired to contribute. You might think this would result in nobody ever coming home because we all want to be third, but it actually works out pretty well. I end up making supper about twice a week, which is my fair share.

Mother had the week's menu taped to the refrigerator. We are pretty flexible about menus. We accept any meal as long as we don't have to make it! I tried to work up enthusiasm for tuna casserole, grilled cheese, or pork chops, but I failed. I poked through the fridge, the shelves, and the cupboards trying to find some thrilling ingredient that would inspire me to make the meal of the month, but I failed.

Both my parents have always worked. Nobody in our family is the least bit domestic, which I think is a pity. I don't want to try it myself, but sometimes I do yearn for the family life that people have in magazines — you know, where they're all out grilling the fish they caught together on the deck they built together, wearing the clothing they stitched together amid the flowers they tended together.

I comfort myself with the thought that at least we Travises are together! We like to talk (my father mostly about politics and the economy; my mother about zoning and religion) and we like to watch TV together. We're not what Ferris refers to as Poster Child America (her previous status) but then, who is?

I had dragged out the Bisquick and was thinking of making hot tuna cheese melt to go on biscuits, maybe with green beans, but I wasn't sufficiently interested to actually start measuring. Kenny, I thought. I wonder if Kenny is a Poster Child.

I didn't know either of his parents, although of course I had seen them. I knew he had an older sister and a younger sister, but they were enough older and younger so that I had never associated with them.

K.K., I thought. Well, I guess there's no point in writing that anywhere. I'll never Keep Kenny. If I had played things right, we could be going to the movies this weekend. But no, I had to throw in basketball. Instead

I'll probably watch the sports channel on cable TV with Dad.

The only movie Kenny and I had seen together was an absolutely horrifying thing about suburban women who are wrenched apart by occult forces and lose their children and lovers to demonic creatures. It was hard to feel romantic during that movie. It was even hard to eat popcorn during that movie. In fact, by the end of the film I was so scared I had forgotten I was even with Kenny.

Tonight I would have to tell my parents about the cafeteria/principal's office/swim pool scenes. My mother would love it about as much as Kenny.

I hoisted the Bisquick box as if it weighed a ton and stared at the proportions of milk to Bisquick. Life is altogether too demanding for me.

"Hello, Pumpkin," said my father, coming in the back door. He kissed me on the forehead. "You haven't started that yet? Good. I'm in the mood for a pizza with everything. Shall I order it?"

"Always," I said. "Pepperoni and mozzarella."

"But I want peppers and anchovies, too."

"Anchovies are disgusting."

My mother came in and kissed us both. "Is this pizza talk? You know I detest pizza."

"How about if I make you leek soup and a grilled provolone cheese on rye?" said my father. "And Tory and I will have pizza."

"Deal," said my mother, kicking off her

high heels. "So, Tory darling, how was school? Anything interesting happen?"

"Well, I went to see Dr. Chafee about making some changes in the athletic department," I said.

My mother was bent over her discarded shoes. Her fingers tightened on the leather. "I thought you weren't going to make any more scenes."

"It wasn't really a scene," I said, although really it had been. I omitted Mike, Aaron, the cafeteria, and the screaming hordes that had accompanied me. "I didn't accomplish much," I said breezily, as if it hardly mattered, "but he did say I had excellent verbal skills and he would mention that to my English teacher."

Nothing like the mention of excellent verbal skills to sidetrack a parent. My father phoned for the pizza and my mother went upstairs to get out of her dress, and I opened the envelope of leek soup mix, and that, for the moment, was that.

Ferris came over after supper. We sat around trying to learn chess. Missile says chess is the most intellectual, most instructive game on earth and we should all master it. I have never been crazy about board games. If I'm tired enough to sit down, I'd rather watch television. "I don't know what to do next," I said.

We consulted the rule book. The trouble with chess is it's a lot more complex than the board games I have conquered — like Sorry

or Parcheesi. "This is as bad as chemistry,"
I said.

"Speaking of chemistry, how's Jonathan?"

"How's *Jonathan*?"

"He's got a crush on you. I'm sure of it."

"Oh, Ferris. Ick. Anyhow, I skipped chemistry today."

"What do you mean, ick? I think Jonathan is neat."

"I think he's a jerk. Anyhow, I'm dating, or at least I think I'm dating Kenny."

"I don't think you are. You don't have any plans for this weekend with him, do you?"

"Best friends are supposed to cheer a person up," I told her.

"I'm miserable because we're moving this week," said Ferris, "and misery loves company. You can't date Kenny. It won't work. You'd have to be sober and calm all the time, conserving your energy and keeping a low profile. Kenny would have to rush around full speed, yelling and cheering to keep up with you. Forget Kenny. You two are not made for each other."

"I don't want to forget Kenny," I told Ferris firmly. "I am not going to forget Kenny. And he isn't going to forget me. This whole thing will smooth over and Kenny and I will be the couple of the year. You'll see."

"Yeah. My mother and father were the couple of the year, too, and now look where they are. Divorced."

"Ferris, would you let me have a fifth date

with Kenny before we begin discussing our divorce?"

"Fifth? You've had only three."

"Four, counting today. The Y."

"That was no date. Kenny had to wait to take you home until that girl Heidi told you all about how awful her tennis courts are. I wouldn't want to escort some girl to her own political convention."

"Ferris, whose side are you on, anyway?"

"Yours," said Ferris. "Sometimes the truth is cruel, Tory, as my mother said when she announced the divorce."

"Aaaaaaaaaahhhh!" I screamed. "Stop it with the divorce talk, Ferris. Enough already!"

"There. Now you know how Kenny feels about the athletic stuff. Enough already."

That really stopped me. If I can irritate Kenny the way Ferris can irritate me, I thought, he never will ask me out again. It's different with best friends. They ride it out because they know things will improve. Kenny doesn't know I'll improve.

"Now, next Monday," said Ferris, "I want you to make a special effort with Jonathan. He watches you all through lunch, and since you share lab with him fifth period every single day, you should be able to get somewhere. Why be dateless when you could be going out with Jonathan?"

"I am not going to be dateless," I said with dignity. "I am going out with Kenny Magnussen." As soon as Ferris left, I began writing K.K. in the corners of everything. Mirror, door, homework, math book. So I wouldn't lose sight of my purpose.

About ten-thirty my mother came in to say good night. "Tory, I had a phone call from Miss L. She says you don't have to bake any brownies for the bake sale. The other girls will do your share." From her voice you would have thought I'd been out robbing old ladies and the rest of the team was going to pay them back for me. "Mom," I said, getting ready to make the big explanation after all.

"I" — she said, in the voice of a martyr — "I will bake those brownies."

"Mom, no. Don't bake anything. We're not going to have a bake sale. You'll see. I just have to talk to the girls a little more about it and they'll understand."

"Understand that you're too lazy to do your share?" she demanded fiercely.

"Mother! I am not lazy. I do too do my share. It's just that bake sales are not the answer."

"Then what *is* the answer?" she said. "For that matter, what is the *question*?"

But I didn't really know anymore.

Seven

A few days later, Ferris was outdoors with her mother in the slush and ice, moving books, clothes, pots, and pans into an apartment that Ferris called a poor substitute for a happy home. *I* was in American history and could only sympathize distantly. All classes had to report to the library for instruction on how to begin our term papers. I loathe library orientation. They've been telling us how to use the card catalogue since third grade. People who have not figured it out by now should retire.

My mind was too busy to listen to anyone, even Miss Ahlquist, whom I like. She's plump and pink and you'd expect her personality to be soft, too, but she's tough. You could snag a sweater on her conversation. She comes to all the basketball games. Last year she gave all four of the graduating seniors on the team a red rose. If she hadn't, the most they would have gotten was a hug from their parents, because the school hardly noticed them at all.

I found a place behind the encyclopedias where I could slump way down and not get caught not listening. I decided that the most efficient way to do my worrying was to worry alternately about Kenny and then about the athletic thing. I considered timing it — you know, five minutes for Kenny, five minutes for basketball, three minutes for Kenny, three minutes for field hockey — but I discovered halfway through the instructions on How to Use Basic Informational Sources that worrying is much more fun without structure.

This can be my new hobby, I thought. Worrying is so portable. So easily picked up. And there's an endless source of cheap material.

By the time we were on to Use of the *Reader's Guide,* I had actually managed to laugh myself into a pretty good frame of mind.

"Hi, Tory," said a quiet voice in my ear. It was Jonathan. We were both wearing blue jeans, white oxford shirts, and navy pullover sweaters. The only difference was that I was wearing two gold chains and dangling gold earrings.

"Hi, Jonathan," I murmured. I read the titles of the books on the shelf above the encyclopedias and studied the label on the jeans of the girl standing in front of me. Miss Ahlquist droned on.

Jonathan took out a felt-tipped pen and an index card. One side of the card was covered with notes about a chemistry assignment. Jonathan turned it to the blank side and slid his pen silently over the paper. He handed it to me. *Enjoyed the treat,* it said.

I had no idea what treat Jonathan could possibly be referring to.

Miss Ahlquist sensed a certain lack of participation from our end of the room and marched over. I shrank, but she chose Jonathan and forced him to demonstrate how to use the *Reader's Guide* to look up the latest articles on Strategic Arms Limitations Talks.

The period ended, as all prison sentences do, and I slouched toward my next class. I told myself that I would bump into Kenny in the hall and he would give me his wide smile, the uncontrolled one, the one that made me feel like a flower blossoming.

"You're certainly an excellent cook," said Jonathan teasingly.

I looked at him blankly.

"Your brownies," he said. "I loved them."

He was talking in riddles.

"At the bake sale," he said, laughing. "For the basketball team. What's the matter, Tory? You trying to operate on five minutes of sleep these days, with all the things you're into?"

"The bake sale?" I repeated. Had my mother baked for me after all? But I had thought the team would talk about it again.

That we would come to an understanding
and —

Jonathan held out a tiny, empty pink plate
wrapped in Saran, tied with a tiny, curling
pink ribbon. *"These* brownies," he explained.
"The invisible ones. I paid fifty cents for
them. It's a terrific gimmick, Tory. I'll be
interested to see how much the team makes
on it."

They had actually done it. They had actually used my name to raise bake sale money.
Written on the empty pink paper plate were
the words: TORY'S FAMOUS INVISIBLE BROWN-
IES. "Oh, that makes me so mad!" I said, taking the plate from Jonathan.

"Why? You have a copyright on your
name?"

"The point was that we have to *stop* having bake sales. The *boys* don't have bake
sales. And it's even worse to make money off
how I feel, as if it's all some big joke." I discovered something about my anatomy. For
me, anger was located in the lungs. It made
my chest hurt and my alveoli prickle and
breathing difficult.

"Tory," complained Jonathan, "you
crushed it." He removed his little pink plate
from my grip. Pink, I thought. Oh, won't
Chafee love this. This is just what he wants
his fine, fine girls to do. Sweetly bake, sweetly
sell, let the boys go on getting the school
money.

"I think it's clever," said Jonathan. "Or it
was till you wrecked it." He looked ruefully

at the crushed Invisible Brownie package in his hand. "See you around, Tory."

As he turned the corner of the corridor, he dropped his Invisible Brownie into the trash basket.

The tears rose up in my eyes. Now I had even alienated Jonathan, who was nobody at all, who didn't even interest me — but who deserved better. Deserved basic courtesy, at least. The tears were hot enough to have been cooked on a flame. They hurt my eyes.

I went down the central stairs two at a time to the foyer where all bake and ticket sales are traditionally held. Missile literally blocked my attack. "Now, Tory. Don't fly off the handle. It's a wonderful idea and already we've raised a hundred and seventy dollars. That's four times as well as we've ever done on a bake sale."

Mary Cat bounced up. "What I think is, Tory," she told me, "that you've already done some good. People are trying to show their support by coming and buying."

No, they weren't. They were just getting a kick out of a gimmick.

Susannah rang up sales of six more Invisible Brownies.

"I'm saving mine," said Peggy, carefully tucking her pink plate into her book bag. "It'll be a real souvenir of the school year, don't you think?"

"Save one for Ferris," said Chrissie. "She'll be absolutely furious that we went and did it on the day she's absent. How's her move going, anyhow, Tory? She seemed to feel pretty good about it, despite her complaining."

"She's glad things are finally happening," said Peggy. "It's the worrying that's rough, not the doing."

It was Peggy knowing what my best friend was going through. And nobody seemed to know what *I* was going through. "But you all missed the point," I said desperately.

"The point is," said Chrissie, "that we showed brilliance in advertising skill and fund raising. Go get some more change, will you, Tory? Instead of just hanging around doing nothing."

I got the change. Then I sat on top of a broken radiator with Susannah and Peggy and listened to them argue about sneakers. Peggy insisted that for good support you should wear high-top sneakers. Susannah believed that we should wear only Nikes, so as to impress the other teams out of their sweat socks. Mary Cat came over and put in for well-ventilated sneakers, whose many years of loving service had rendered them gray from use, and nicely sprinkled with holes, and hung with frayed laces.

"Okay, girls," said Missile. "Fold up the card tables and eat those unsold cookies. Time for practice."

"They're whole-wheat cookies," said Mary Cat. "They're ghastly." But she ate one anyway and handed me another. They tasted interesting, but not good.

"Tory," said Missile, putting her arm around me, "I knew you were too tough to get beaten down by a passing mood. Now get a smile going."

I smiled and she clapped me on the back. "We're up against Western on Thursday," she said, "and when we win we'll be number one. So let's really *work* today."

But we didn't work. We crept around, taking no chances, conserving our energy, worrying about something. It's me, I thought. I've done something. I've destroyed something. This isn't basketball, it's Nerf ball.

I felt dried out. Brittle. I couldn't seem to do anything and the harder I tried the worse I got. Every time I remembered that we were playing this very Thursday, I'd get tense instead of excited and play badly. When Missile said, "*When* we win" instead of "*If* we win," I would think: If I don't shape up, we'll lose. Which increased the old anxiety level until I couldn't even catch a simple pass.

Nobody said anything.

Finally Missile took me out and put one of the JV girls in. An eighth grader. She played twice as well.

I sat on the bottom bleacher, the only one pulled out, so that I had a twelve-foot-high backrest, and I struggled against tears. I could not believe myself. Without me things went better. I had been an obstruction to my own team.

"An awesome shot," said Chrissie to Peggy. "Truly awesome."

"Whaddaya mean?" said Mary Cat. "She missed by about a mile."

"True, but a vertical mile. When you have to get reports from Houston Air Control," said Chrissie, "to locate the ball, it is a truly awesome miss."

Susannah retrieved the ball. "Peggy," she said ominously, "there is frost on this ball."

"Probably threw it all the way to Iowa," said Chrissie.

"Forget Iowa," said Peggy. "All I care about is beating Western."

And then, wonderfully, mysteriously, that was all I cared about, too. Money, bake sales, splinters, puddles — I didn't care about any of it. I just wanted to play, be back on the team, do my share, and whip Western on Thursday. I stood up and yelled and clapped and basically did the rah-rah bit for the rest of the girls until Missile decided my attitude was okay again and she put me back in.

It was an incredible relief to be doing nothing but playing ball. Not worrying about it, not agonizing over it — just playing. (Though why it's called playing I don't know; it's *work*.)

"Look at that jump!" yelled Peggy. "That woman is a gazelle!"

Mary Cat turned with a very ungazelle-like expression. "I," she said, "am a panther and don't you forget it."

Susannah managed to steal the ball, Peggy got a little too anxious to get it back, and

Missile called a foul. Susannah loves foul shots. She almost never misses, whether it's practice or a game. She bounces the ball five times first. Not four. Not six. Just five. Then she shoots.

She sank both of them, of course, perfectly, and we cheered like Julie's crowd, waving invisible pom-pons.

Invisible Brownies, I thought, and I laughed. It was a cute idea. I was glad they'd gone ahead and done it.

Peggy threw the ball in, Mary Cat intercepted, pivoted, tossed to Susannah, and Susannah threw it — but it struck the rim. With a war whoop I flung myself up, spanked the ball sideways, and sent it right back into the net.

. . . And the double doors to the gym opened.

It was the Kennedy boys' wrestling team.

Missile blew her whistle.

"Okay, girls," said the Kennedy coach cheerfully, "we'll give you five. Then we need your locker rooms."

We plowed to a halt, glaring at the boys, and the usual undercurrent of muttered protests began.

"Five," muttered Mary Cat. "It takes me ten minimum to shower and fix my horrible hair. Where does he get off, giving us five?"

"Who's the cute one on the left?" said Chrissie. "He can share a locker with me anytime."

"I hate surrendering my own locker room to the visiting team," said Susannah darkly. "Dumb boys."

"Let's move it, girls," called Missile. "Their match is scheduled for four-thirty. Terrific practice, absolutely the best ever. I know we're going to win Thursday!"

"You'd think at least your own locker room could be private," said Mary Cat. "The Tampax machine is out, too. Can't you just hear the remarks from these jocks when they see that."

"In Iowa," started Peggy. But I wasn't listening.

My hand turned to ice. All over me the sweat prickled and shivered.

Where is it written that the way to make things work is for the girls to give things up?

The Kennedy boys slouched across the gym floor, their gym bags held loosely in their hands, waiting for us to leave our own gym.

"No," I said.

Everyone heard.

All the girls. All the boys. Both coaches.

There was a strange, slow-motion swivel, and all of them turned and looked at me. My skin crawled with nerves. Everybody looked so far away. So remote. "No," I repeated. "We're having an important practice. We have a big game coming up. We're not giving up the gym and we're not giving up our locker room. Go change in the boys' locker room with the other team. Or go down the hall and use the bathroom. For all I care, you can change in the hall."

One by one the Kennedy boys flushed and began backing away from me. I stood very still and stared them down. Their coach was frozen with astonishment. I took one step forward — and all those big, muscular jocks took one step back.

I'm going to win, I thought. A good offense, and all that.

Very quietly Missile said, "Come on, Tory."

I stared at her.

"Tory, this is how things work. I'm sorry, too. I'd like to continue our practice. But we can't."

Goose pimples rose all up and down my bare arms. My *hair* hurt, as if it was attached to my scalp with pins. "Missile," I whispered, "whose side are you on?"

The Kennedy coach came up and put an arm like a deer carcass around my shoulders. "Got a little women's lib going on here, huh?" He laughed hugely.

I would have kicked him in the shins and stomped on him, or at the very least bitten his arm, but Missile just smiled courteously. "Hello, Arthur," she said. "Yes, indeed. And more where this came from. However, we will allow you to have the gym today as scheduled." Her fingers tightened on my arm as if I were a tennis racket she was fixing. "Let's go, Tory."

The wrestling team was staring at me.

Some looked amused and some annoyed. A few looked as if they would rather be anywhere than near that crazy girl with the basketball.

My team had not moved from where they were on the court. They had not advanced on the boys with me, or said anything to support me — but they had not moved away from me, either. Now they waited for me, and as I reached each one, Missile's arm forcing me, they joined, until we became a sort of chorus line. Silently we filed into our locker room. Back in the gym the Kennedy boys began laughing.

"Tory!" said Mary Cat between her teeth. "I agree with you, but don't make these scenes without asking the rest of us if that's what we want to do! I'm not going to leave you alone out there — I'm the captain and this is a team. But how dare you start that without even asking the rest of us?"

"I'm sorry." I was not sorry. I was burning again. Raging.

Chrissie said slowly, admiringly, "You're tough, Tory. I wouldn't have stood up to them. You almost pulled it off."

"I *could* have pulled it off if Missile hadn't interfered."

"It's not that easy," said Missile.

"Why not?" I was screaming and I knew it but I couldn't seem to stop. In the corner of my eye I saw Peggy check to be sure the heavy door was all the way shut — to keep my screaming private. "What's so hard about it?" I demanded. "It doesn't take any time at all to make the visiting boys use the boys' locker room instead of ours. Would it kill the two teams to change together? It wouldn't take any money, either. Oh, Missile, why don't you do anything? What's the matter with you? How come you didn't stick up for me out there? You *know* it isn't fair!"

My tears spilled over. There was nothing to wipe them up with but an old sock lying on the bench.

"Tory, I have to keep the respect and friendships of the other coaches and teachers. If I don't, I can't accomplish one single thing. Wrecking the game schedules of the entire athletic region is not the way to begin."

"Begin," I repeated sarcastically. "You've been here four years now, Missile. How can you talk about beginning?" I hated myself for screaming at Missile. I hated all my anger and loneliness and failure. I hated the way the rest of the team was looking at me, as if I were a freak they had to put up with.

Missile gave me a raw, hurt look. Like Kenny that day in the parking lot. As if I'd thrown something sharp in her face.

Oh, Kenny, I thought wildly, Kenny, what have I done? I was going to keep you. Kenny, don't be angry with me.

But if my friends and my team were disgusted with me, I could not expect Kenny to be otherwise.

"Four years ago," said Missile, "we didn't get one line of newspaper coverage on girls' sports. We couldn't even get the intramural schedules printed to be passed out in school, let alone printed in the city paper. We had a swimming champion the year I first came here, Tory. She set school records, regional records, and two state records. And do you know how often she was written up in the paper? Twice. *Twice*."

There were tears in Missile's eyes. It chilled me: the way you'd feel if you saw your parents crying, or the president. *Missile* crying.

"Tory, it took me two years to convince the editors of the sports pages that people would read about girls, too. Now we get calendars of coming events, the occasional photograph, the interview once in a while. We've even had a stringer cover games if we're close to the finals. Tory, I'm the first to agree I haven't accomplished much. But I'm trying."

Beyond her tears were ragged edges. She was torn and bruised from being alone in a fight.

"Now look what you've done, Tory!" snapped Susannah. "Now Missile's crying."

"I'm sorry," I whispered. I'm sorry, Missile. I'm sorry, Kenny. I'm sorry, Mom.

Mary Cat said unexpectedly, "Tory didn't start a thing, Susannah. She just noticed it, that's all. We've all noticed it. And we've all bitched about it. It's just that up till now we've chosen to dismiss it because we don't want to deal with it."

Why worry about Kenny? I thought. He

hasn't bothered with me since the day at the Y, anyhow. "So now we can deal with it?" I said hesitantly.

"Not like that," said Missile. "Unless I keep on the good side of the men, we won't get anything."

"I would not want the friendship of people like him," I said.

Missile shrugged. I wondered what it was like to work with coaches like Arthur, always taking your time, your space, your team, your share of the money. "I'm sorry I yelled at you, Missile."

"Don't be sorry. I'm proud of you." She hugged me, but it was an empty hug. A hug with despair in it. We dressed slowly. I could feel her hug with every button I buttoned.

One by one the girls filed out. They touched me, leaving. There's something about teams that makes you touch. Fingertips. Palms. As though what's between you is too basic for words.

"Missile," I said.

"Aren't you dressed yet, Tory? Hurry up. The boys are banging on the door." Missile shook her head, gathered up the rest of my things, and pulled me into her office. "Come on in, guys," she yelled. "All clear." She shut the door on us. Her office was like a locker: gray, narrow, vertical, ugly.

"What shall I do next?" I said.

Missile pulled back from me, amazed, as if it had never crossed her mind that I would do something else. It hadn't crossed my mind, either, until I felt her despair. I felt as if we *had* to do something together — and yet I knew I was the only one ready to do anything at all. K.K., I thought. Well, that's down the tubes. I may as well plunge back in.

"I guess," Missile said slowly, "you should talk to Mr. Giametti. He's the head of the athletic department. You really should have gone to him first instead of Dr. Chafee. People get offended when you don't go in the right order." She hesitated and touched my hair. "Mr. Giametti is not easy to deal with."

No doubt she had had a lot of opportunity to learn this. I tied my shoelaces. "That," I said, "makes two of us."

E^{ight}

Everyone from Missile to me is a bit afraid of Mr. Giametti. He's not tall. He may not even be as tall as I am. But he's wide. It's as if somebody put a building on the Incredible Hulk's head and squashed him down and out. Great shuddering arms swing like wrecking balls from rippling shoulders. When Mr. Giametti lowers himself in their direction, chairs appear to be made of toothpicks. So when I said, "Who wants to go with me to talk to Mr. Giametti?" Ferris, Peggy, Chrissie, and Susannah all burst out laughing.

"Plan A," said Ferris, "is save thy skin."

"He won't skin me," I retorted.

"I wouldn't be too sure," said Ferris.

I sat through my classes eyeing people, wondering if any of them were Facing Mr. Giametti types. Or even Associating with Tory Travis types.

But I didn't see anyone.

Mary Cat said, "Listen, Tory. I don't know if I approve of all this. But — but I guess it's wrong for you to go alone. I — I don't want to do any of the talking." She flushed and looked feverish. "But I'll come."

"Thanks, Mary Cat."

She shrugged.

After school, I watched people pouring onto buses and into cars. I felt like the only rat too dumb to leave the sinking ship. Ferris tapped my shoulder. "Ferris," I said, surprised. "I thought you were taking the bus."

"I'll take the late bus. If you're going in to see Mr. Giametti I guess I'd better come, too. I'm supposed to be your best friend, you know. Some best friend, letting you go alone to your execution."

"He's not going to execute me, Ferris."

Ferris sniffed. "This is not good judgment coming from a girl who wants to date Kenny Magnussen."

"Shut up, Ferris," I said. I wished I had never told her a single word about Kenny, a single dream. I had always liked it before that Ferris and I could see inside each other; it was comforting. Now I regretted it. What she could see was private.

Kenny. If he were a real boyfriend — or even a real friend — I would have asked him to come face Mr. Giametti. But I could not imagine him in an assault position. I could see him as a commentator, or a spectator, or an arranger — but not a player.

Funny, I thought. A month ago I saw

Kenny every time I turned around. Before school, between class, after school. Now I never see him at all. He's the Invisible Brownie. First whiff of trouble and he's gone.

But that wasn't fair. This was not Kenny's war. It was nobody's war but mine.

That, at least, was depressingly clear.

However, there was no way for Giametti to know just how lukewarm my support really was. Mary Cat and Ferris were coming from guilt, not conviction. But maybe any reason is as good as another.

I put Kenny to the side. He was like an object, somehow, that I could tuck away and take out again when I needed it, like a dog worrying an old shoe.

Oh, poor Kenny, I thought, laughing, being compared to an old shoe.

The discussion began with Mr. Giametti giving me a look that would freeze penguins. I'll give Mary Cat credit. She looked at Giametti with the same victorious boredom she uses on teams we're about to confront. Ferris, who likes people to be friends (especially when they're her parents), stared at the spine of a book on coaching that lay on Giametti's desk. I knew she was pretending to be somewhere else.

This time, at least, I had rehearsed what I was going to say. I didn't stumble or whine. I stated the problems, listed the inequities, and then waited.

It was hard to look at Mr. Giametti. His

face was covered with the remnants of a terrible complexion he'd had back in the Dark Ages when he was my age. I ended up staring at my little written list, or at Mary Cat's elegant profile, or at my tote bag dumped on the floor. My quilt square, my math workbook, and my gym suit poked out of it.

"Have you," said Mr. Giametti, "registered these complaints with your gym teacher?"

You would have thought Lockridge High had dozens of women's gym teachers, whose names and faces were easily forgotten by the busy athletic director. "Yes, Mr. Giametti."

He picked up a yellow pencil and began rolling it between his hands. Then he put one hand at each end and pressed gently. The pencil did not break. It would, though, when he felt like snapping it.

"And did she suggest," said Giametti, "that the next step was to talk to me?" He made it sound as if Missile were recommending Molotov cocktails instead of basketballs.

The pencil curved.

I decided to keep poor Missile out of it. "She said I would have to follow my conscience."

Clearly Mr. Giametti was not crazy about people following their consciences. He frowned. On his massive forehead a frown resembled a newly plowed field. He could hold a pencil in the wrinkles of his frown. I was so anxious I began to giggle under my breath, and I had to choke myself to keep Giametti from noticing. I sounded like someone who needed adrenalin for an asthma attack.

"If playing on a team is so upsetting for you," he said at last, "perhaps you should solve things by dropping out."

I think my temperature dropped about ten degrees. I could feel ice in my veins. Dropping out? Quitting the team?

Giametti smiled, but the frown stayed. "I'm afraid your lack of perspective and consideration is quite damaging to the rest of the team, Tory."

I could think of nothing to say. My tongue hurt, trying to move it around, trying to form words. I really am going to have an asthma attack, I thought, my breath coming quicker and quicker, the distress rising to the surface like a rubber ball in the water.

Giametti turned to Mary Cat and Ferris, who were clearly representing the rest of the girls.

I have to hand it to Mary Cat. Or maybe to basketball. You don't play out in public, making your errors and your misses and your fumbles in front of hundreds of people, without developing quite a lot of poise. You don't become captain of a team without being able to dish it out and take it, too. Mary Cat said, "On the contrary, Mr. Giametti, Tory's efforts have made the rest of us think."

The smile vanished and the two halves of his face matched again: frowns. He did not like the picture of girls thinking. He said to me, "You don't think this might disrupt your playing and your concentration? To be focusing on other things at a crucial time like this?"

Ferris, no doubt remembering practice, winced. Giametti saw her and was glad. Mary Cat looked remote and elegant — and distant.

I struggled for control. I looked back down at my list. What if he was right? What if I did damage my team? We were almost sure to be regional champions; we were certain to do very well, if not the best, in the state play-offs. What if I played on Thursday the way I'd played at practice? What if they had to put a JV girl in for me? "It isn't just the basketball team," I said, my fingers so tight on the list that it curled around my fingers like hair. "The hockey sticks. You can't grip them properly. The tennis courts. They need new nets."

Mr. Giametti got up from his desk and walked around it to me. I thought he would stab me with the pencil, but instead he sat on the edge of his desk, right up next to me, and he leaned down, so that his awful, puckered face was shoved into mine. He said nothing.

I shivered, and he saw that, too, and was glad. "What you are suggesting, Tory," said Mr. Giametti, "is the introduction of mediocrity into a fine athletic department. If I diluted the funds going into my football and basketball teams, just to give you girls

Twinkies and monogrammed towels, we'd be losers."

He was making it sound as though I was being frivolous and silly, like a little cheerleader wanting fluffier pom-pons!

Mary Cat said in a thin, rather harsh voice, "I don't seem to recall Tory suggesting Twinkies and monogrammed towels."

He bared his teeth at her in what he may have thought was a smile. "I'm not exaggerating any more than Tory is. Now the answer to every single one of your requests is this, girls: *No*."

Ferris flinched.

My head ached fiercely.

Mary Cat looked thin and aristocratic.

"And Tory," said Mr. Giametti softly, opening the door for us to leave, "don't try wrecking my relationships with visiting schools again, huh? Don't even think about it."

Ferris said, "No, sir."

I said nothing.

This time three of us stood in the white tiles and blinked in the shiny bathrooms and put wet paper towels on our foreheads.

"There," said Ferris. "You've gotten it out of your system, Tory. You've carried it as far as you can and you've got your answer. He made it quite, quite clear." She wet another towel, pressed it down with her two palms over her eyes, as if trying to bruise them. " '*No*,' " she quoted. "Lord, I hate scenes. That made me think of my mother and father. All that quiet, held-in screaming."

There was a long silence. Finally I looked at Mary Cat. I have never felt close to her. She's a senior and very proud of it. She's captain and even prouder of that. And there's something about her, that cool elegance, that makes me feel thick and dull. She has a way of removing herself from things, being inaccessible, as though she had no part in it, was just passing by. I never feel that way. I always feel caught up in things, a net around me.

Mary Cat's eyes fluttered and she said very quietly, "I don't think senior year is going to be what I expected."

"What do you mean?" said Ferris.

"I mean I won't have it."

I knew what she meant. Ferris did not. Ferris said, "Huh?"

"I won't have that man looking at us that way and refusing things," said Mary Cat. "Refusing even the things that are sensible. That could easily be done."

"They can't be done *now*," said Ferris. "The season is practically over. Anyhow, you're graduating. You don't have to get involved."

Mary Cat said, "I felt something queer in there. I felt as though I owed a debt. This school has given me everything. I've loved it here. Maybe I should give the school something in return."

Ferris cried, "Oh, Mary Cat, stop it! Stop getting half crazed like Tory! All you'll do is get the whole team hurt. Just forget it!"

"No," said Mary Cat.

Ferris' mother picked her up, but Mary Cat and I declined a ride. We sat in Missile's office, talking. Mary Cat has a key to it. Missile wasn't there, but we could feel her. Calm and decent and trying — and failing. We sat while it got dark, and Mary Cat held a basketball in her hands, rubbing her thumbs over the tiny, gravelly nubs on its surface, bouncing it now and then. And we talked.

When we finally decided we'd better head home, the sky was completely gray, as if it had never seen sunshine and never would — just molten steel untouched by pleasure. We walked home.

"You're stomping the pavement as if it's Giametti's face," I said to Mary Cat.

"The pavement is more attractive," she said.

A block from the school the sidewalks vanished and we walked in slush and wet grass and old, blackened snow. "I can't think of anything to do," I said. "If the principal says no, and the athletic director says no, and our coach is at a dead end, then what can we actually *do*?" I looked up at the sky, hoping for relief — for something beautiful and eternal. Far to the west was a penciled line in the gray. Was it the wingspread of a hawk a mile away, or a jet trail at the back of the horizon?

A car sprayed me and I moved behind Mary Cat and walked on the grass. The pencil line was a *V* of geese. A lopsided *V*. As it came closer I saw four geese on one angle of the *V* and about fifty on the other. It seemed to me that the four must be working much harder against the wind than the fifty, who were just sailing along in each other's wake.

The geese were screaming at each other: loud, sore-throated croaks. Mary Cat said, "What would happen if the leader gave up? Do you suppose the next goose in line would take over? Or would they just land? Wait for tomorrow, when maybe Goose Number One will have it all together again?"

We watched the *V* till it vanished from sight. Nobody changed sides. The hard-working geese kept working hard and the hangers-on kept hanging.

We reached Mary Cat's road long before mine. "I'll call you if I think of anything," she said, but both of us knew we were out of thoughts.

"Okay. Thanks for going in with me, Mary Cat."

She nodded and walked alone down her street. I had another two miles to go. Good exercise, I told myself. But I felt as if I were on a leash, being dragged. I had an ally now, and a powerful one: Few seniors were more illustrious than Mary Cat. But neither of us had the slightest idea what to do, so nothing had changed.

I was crying. The wind blew fiercely and it hurt where the tears lay, as if tears had weakened my skin. Cars threw ice water on me. I slid in a slush puddle and soaked my feet. I smudged the tears up with my jacket sleeve and later on I used the same sleeve for a Kleenex. Why am I even doing this? I thought. I've upset my best friend, angered my mother, and lost my second chance to date Kenny.

Kenny.

If I were walking with Kenny, the sky wouldn't be gray. I wouldn't notice the slush nor feel the wind. We would share my mitten and his fingers would close over mine and we would be talking about us, and about happy things.

"Tory!"

A car ground to a halt next to me. For an instant, still half blind from tears, I thought — Kenny. He worried about me, he came after me, he —

But it was neither a white Datsun nor a red Corvette. It was a very beat-up, dark green station wagon, and when the passenger door opened Gwynne Yardley leaned out, yelling for me to hop in and they would give me a ride home.

They meaning Gwynne and her boyfriend ... Dusty.

I hardly know Gwynne. She is the kind of

girl who edits the literary magazine, while I am the one who doesn't even buy it. She is the one who takes four years of Latin while I am the one who thinks it's a real hardship to take two of French.

If Gwynne ever had any exercise in her life except for numbering the pages of her brilliant term papers, I didn't know about it. Gwynne was always the last girl chosen in gym for any team and she never even cared.

"Get in!" yelled Dusty. "There are cars piling up behind me!"

Gwynne scooted over next to Dusty to make room in the front seat for me. "Thanks," I said. I kept my face toward the window, so they wouldn't see the tears tracked down my cheeks.

"Your feet are soaked," remarked Gwynne. "Pull off your sneakers and we'll aim the heat vents at your feet."

I just sat there, though, hanging onto my tote bag and wishing I could quilt Mr. Giametti's lips.

Dusty pulled up in front of the drive-in window at the Burger King. At first I thought it was torture for me — but he was just hungry. "You want something, Tory?" he said, placing orders for himself and Gwynne.

I had about fifty cents. "Coke," I said.

Dusty ordered me a hamburger and fries.

"Dusty —" I began.

"You're frozen," he pointed out. "Frozen people need hot food."

"Yes, but I'm broke," I said.

the precise purpose of this crusade, Tory?"

"It isn't a crusade. It isn't even a purpose. It's just that things aren't fair and I want something done."

Gwynne shook her head fiercely about eighteen times.

"She does that to look intelligent," Dusty explained to me. "She's trying to get the stagnant molecules in her gray matter moving around and functioning."

Gwynne shoved a French fry in his face and he ate it, grinning. I had this terrible, painful surge of jealousy. Not envy. Not something small and shruggish the way you'd feel about a nicer sweater or a better vacation. But jealousy. Terrible and wicked and hot. *I* wanted to be the one with the terrific boyfriend. *I* wanted to be the one laughing, sure of myself, making jokes.

With Kenny.

"Give me your facts," said Gwynne firmly.

I gave her my facts.

"Those aren't facts," said Gwynne scornfully. "Those are complaints. Where are your *facts*?"

"Oh, good grief," I cried. "What facts? I'm supposed to estimate how many ice cream sundaes Mrs. Fargo has bought us as opposed to how many free meals the cafeteria has packed for the boys? I'm supposed to do a survey on how many girls have actually gotten splinters in their palms from using old hockey sticks?"

"Attendance," said Gwynne. "Participation. Square footage. Dollars. Dollars. Dollars. You have to compile the statistics of the true situation."

"And then what? Mr. Giametti would just as soon sell me into slavery as listen to the statistics of the true situation, Gwynne."

Gwynne tilted her chin up. She finished her bit of burger. She set down her oozing ketchup package. "Then," she said softly, looking down her nose at me and nodding another ten times, "you publish."

Nine

All night long, while my parents watched a movie on Home Box Office, I wandered around the house muttering to myself.

"Publish?" I said to the refrigerator. "What does she mean — publish?"

My mother's little magnet that says: I'M NOT FAT — JUST SHORT FOR MY WEIGHT looked back at me with its smiley face.

"She thinks I'm going to write a book?" I demanded. I got out an English muffin and split it. "Listen. It's all I can do to write a paragraph on an English test." I spread some leftover spaghetti sauce on the muffin and sprinkled a little grated cheese over that. "She wants me to publish something about the girls' athletic department at Lockridge," I mumbled, shoving the little pizzas into the toaster oven and putting it on Top Brown. "Oh, right. I can see the Book of the Month Club snapping it up right now."

For English homework I had to write an analysis of a poem by John Donne. I reread it. "This is probably the stupidest, most illiterate piece of writing ever done," I said to my pizza crust. "And Gwynne Yardley wants to whip the athletic department with the power of *my* pen? Hah!"

It was nine-thirty before Gwynne called. "What took you so long?" I demanded. "Anyhow, it doesn't matter. I've been thinking about your idea and it's ridiculous. It wouldn't work. I can't even write. And who's going to read it?"

"Everybody," said Gwynne. "Now. I've called a special meeting of the literary magazine staff. Tomorrow morning in the library before school."

She wanted to publish in the *literary magazine*? Now I had heard everything. "Gwynne, I don't think —"

"They're all frustrated reporters," said Gwynne. "Did you know Lockridge High used to have a twice-weekly newspaper? Really. But about ten years ago the students got very political and antiwar and pro-something else and the principal sold the presses."

"I didn't know that. But —"

"It's true. Someday we'll have to start up another paper."

"Gwynne!" I beat a tattoo on the bare floor with my bedroom slippers. If there was one thing I did not plan to do with my junior year, it was start a newspaper.

"Be quiet and listen," said Gwynne. "We're going to print a position paper. We'll pass it out in school. Enough copies for every single student and one for them to take home to their parents."

"A position paper?" I said dubiously.

"On discrimination against girls in the athletic department of Lockridge Senior High. Be there, Tory. Otherwise, we won't know what our position is."

A position paper, I thought. It certainly sounds official.

My parents came out of the TV room looking happy and confused, the way you feel after a really super movie, when it transported you so completely that the popcorn stands and the pushy people come as something of a shock.

As casually as possible, I said, "Gwynne and Mary Cat and I and some others are going to write a position paper on the athletic department and distribute it around the school."

The whole idea flew through me like wind: the idea of it, getting the kids behind us, maybe not the power of the pen so much as the power of the student body. Eleven hundred kids all wanting the same thing. Now *that* would shake up Giametti and Chafee!

My mother said woodenly, "You know I don't care for this kind of thing, Tory."

"Mom, please. Let me explain."

"I'm not interested. Explain it to your father." She went upstairs without saying good night. The exuberance came out of me like water from a plastic bag. I stood there wilted and wrinkled.

When Mom closed the bedroom door behind her, Dad put his arm around me. "Do what you have to do, Pumpkin," he said softly. "Don't worry about your mother. She'll weather this."

"Why's she so upset with me?"

"She went back to work ten years ago convinced she'd be a real whiz kid. Shake up the management. Run her own show. But she's still a secretary. No matter what she does, no matter how she tries, she doesn't get past it. Changing companies, changing bosses, changing attitudes — none of it has worked for her. She feels whipped."

I felt a kind of agony for my mother, and at the same time a kind of wrath: How could she never have shared that with me? How could she have gone through all that and never given me a clue? What kind of family were we, that we hid such important things from each other, shared only triumph and never pain?

"I guess" — said my father slowly — "I guess she *is* whipped. It hurts her. She doesn't want you to get hurt and she doesn't see anything else out there for you, Tory."

"Is that what you think?"

He hesitated. "You'll get your share of hurt, I imagine. But there are laws in your favor. I'm not very familiar with them, but it's against the law to discriminate in any institution using federal funds and, believe me, the school uses a lot of federal money. You can't discriminate against anyone on the basis of race, creed, religion, or sex, and if you can prove that the girls are being discriminated against, then you've got a case."

A case. It sounded like a bad rerun on TV. Honorable private eyes against a wicked world. "But Dad," I said, "aren't there laws in Mom's favor, too?"

"Sure. But you don't always win, sweetheart. You know that from basketball. Being right doesn't always matter. Sometimes the stronger team comes out on top and that's that."

He'd been standing behind me, half rocking me against his chest and now he turned me slowly around. He's quite a lot taller than I am. I always hoped I'd be my father's height and not my mother's, but I've reached my growth now and I guess five eight is all I'll ever be.

He kissed my hair. "Just because one person doesn't make it," he said, "is no reason for the next person to surrender without a fight. I'm proud of you and I think you should keep going. And if you were to accomplish something, it would have a bonus for us."

"What?"

"It would give your mother the strength to try again."

I thought about it all night. That I, her daughter, could do something to give her strength. It's the other way around. Your mother picks you up and dusts you off and puts on the Band-Aids and finds the aspirin.

I wanted to telephone Ferris to talk about it, but it was too late at night. Besides, she was only willing to talk about *her* problems. If we moved into mine, she'd hang up so fast she'd get a friction burn on her wrist.

I stared at the white extension phone by my bed and thought of dialing Kenny. Kenny, I would say, I understand my parents. I understand struggling and pain and anxiety. I just grew up a little. I could almost measure it, like on one of those charts you hang on the wall to mark off a little kid's height. Tonight was a whole centimeter.

And Kenny would say, I know just what you mean, Tory.

And I would say, I miss you, Kenny. Let's do something special tomorrow.

And Kenny would say —

I sighed. Kenny would say, Stop this, Tory. You're hysterical. You're making glaciers out of ice cubes again.

Oh, Kenny, I thought. I touched the pillow, wishing it was Kenny, that I could touch him as easily. And knowing he was lost, and it was my own fault.

And if I lose with the athletic thing, too? I thought. If this position paper goes over as well as my talks with Chafee and Giametti, what then? How much worse will that make Mom?

Two generations in a row.
Squashed.

When you get eleven people to the high school at seven-fifteen in the morning, either they must be very dedicated types, or you must have a good cause.

I was absolutely amazed to see the ones who had come. Dusty was there. I knew Dusty was Gwynne's boyfriend and I knew he was sympathetic, but I never guessed he agreed with me in the principle of the thing. He was *captain* of the boys' team. Friend of Aaron and Mike.

"I hadn't ever stopped to think about it before," said Dusty with an apologetic shrug. "But it's true. We get better game scheduling, more practice time at better hours, free meals and drinks and snacks. We get the bus, we get the printed game programs, and the free medical checks. And I agree with you. It's not fair."

One of the boys was Jonathan. I was surprised. We hadn't spoken since that day in the library, other than in chemistry class. I always thought of him as the dippy cello player who's afraid of test tubes and beakers. I've never even been very polite to Jonathan. And here he had drawn this terrific cartoon to illustrate the paper. It showed a group of boys staggering around with huge loads of dollars and footballs and goalie equipment on their backs . . . and the girls darting after them, scavenging for the occasional dollar or flat soccer ball that fell to the ground.

Mary Cat had lined up the senior contingent, but I didn't know most of them, except from afar. So it was impossible for me to know if this was in or out of character for the seniors.

Julie, the cheerleader who had sneered at me, was there. "Julie?" I said in disbelief.

"I've thought about it," she said, half embarrassed and half defiant, "and you're right. Things aren't fair."

"But you're a cheerleader," I protested. I suppose it was a stupid remark, but I have this stereotype about cheerleaders: rah-rah types whose idea of athletics is a bounce to applause.

"That's why," said Julie. "I am so sick of people saying, 'Oh, you're a cheerleader,' and then giggling. As if it's something asinine. Well, it's not. I am perfectly capable of thought and I am also an athlete, although you choose to think that hours of dancing and rehearsing formations and leading hundreds of people in cheers isn't athletic. I happen to be —"

"We can argue about the virtues of cheerleading another time," said Gwynne, and such was the force of her personality that Julie shut up. "Now, this is my plan. We're going to compose this paper in a *Do you know?* style." She had the first example done and we all crowded around to see it.

* * *

Did you know?
> That the boys get free sweat suits?
> Free practice clothing?
> Free competition outfits for both team
>   and individual sports?

Did you know?
> That the girls have to supply their
>   own clothes?

"Oh, that's good," said Mary Cat excitedly, and immediately dictated the next *Do you know?* I tossed out a third. One more idea and we'd consumed the entire first page. I was a little thrown. I had thought we'd have space to say more.

Jonathan and Dusty got into a heated argument over what else to print, since we could use only two sides of one page, and we were already half done. "Tory," said Dusty at last, "you decide. It's your show."

And they all turned and looked at me and waited.

What a feeling! Power, I guess, and pride, and excitement. A hurtling sensation: like going down the Flume at the amusement park. Rushing ahead, really *rushing,* to get things done.

We had to work fast, because a lot of kids had first-period classes. The sheer speed of dictating it, seeing it take shape, seeing my ideas and thoughts form on the page, align themselves, turn into an argument, was really exciting.

"We haven't got many facts," said Jonathan dubiously. "Do you think we should wait until we've done some research? This is good, but it's emotional."

"Of course it's emotional," snapped Gwynne. "This is an emotional topic."

"I'm only saying that statistics, dollars, that kind of thing, look good on a paper like this. And we don't have them."

"Don't need them," said Gwynne airily.

"But when you talked to me about this yesterday," I protested, "that was what you wanted."

Gwynne was annoyed. Clearly she expected to be able to change her mind when she felt like it and the rest of us should obediently change with her. I didn't argue anymore. She was the literary type, not me, and anyhow, "research" sounded like something I would not like, and it was definitely something I didn't know how to start. And if we postponed the paper till this "research" was done, we'd never get the action going again. This was like a game: You play when you're fired up, not when you're bored and acting under orders.

Gwynne startled me by saying exactly the same thing. "Besides," she announced, "we have to strike while the iron is hot."

"What does that mean?" said Mary Cat.

"It means Tory's in the spotlight now. Everybody knows what she's been up to. Hanging around digging up dry facts isn't going to help. More action is what's going to help. Now. I think we'll need about ten thousand copies of this."

"That may be a bit optimistic," said Jonathan, "considering there are eleven hundred students in our school."

Gwynne gave him a look that would chill wine, but Jonathan just grinned and said he thought fifteen hundred would be plenty. Otherwise the extras would just end up as litter all over the school grounds.

"We will write this position paper in such an exciting fashion," said Gwynne icily, "that no on will even *consider* parting with it."

"Right on, Gwynne," said Jonathan, laughing.

I suddenly realized something about Jonathan — he wasn't afraid of anything. Not Gwynne, not Chafee, not Giametti. He didn't do chemistry because he didn't feel like it. He was a Facing Giametti type — and all along I'd thought he was a wimp.

"I looked it up," said Mary Cat.

"Looked what up?" said Gwynne.

"The law. Miss Ahlquist helped me." Mary Cat read it aloud. It was called Title IX and the introductory paragraph, which we used to close our position paper, said, "No person in the United States shall, on the basis of sex, be excluded from participation in, be denied the benefits of, or be subject to discrimination under, any education program or activity receiving federal assistance."

"Not bad," said Dusty. "A nationwide law. I didn't even know about it."

"I could have told you anytime," said Gwynne with a sniff.

"Okay, Tory," said Julie, separating the syllables like in a cheer, and she whacked my back.

I was a ship with my sails full of wind. I floated out of the meeting and into class. During the whole day — gym, practice, lunch, classes — I was swirling with what was happening.

We were on the road.

Ten

Thursday morning.

Seven-thirty.

The student parking lot was beginning to fill. The first bus was due in five minutes. "Okay, people," said Gwynne, grinning, feverish with excitement, "man your stations."

"Woman them, you mean," said Julie.

We all giggled, even the boys. Mary Cat and her crew were handling the band-room basement entrance and the east door, which is an EXIT ONLY, but all the kids with homerooms down that way use it for an entrance, anyhow. Jonathan and I were handling the front foyer. Gwynne and Dusty took the parking lot and Julie's people the central stairwell.

I hoisted my sheaf of position papers and stood by the huge fingerprint-marred front doors, ready to pass my knowledge and wisdom to all comers.

The school will be knocked on its ear! I thought exultantly. Dr. Chafee's eyebrows will freeze into position. Once he reads this, he'll see he should have listened to me. Probably I'll get interviewed by the newspaper: HIGH SCHOOL JUNIOR MAKES WAVES. TOWN SHOCKED AT CONDITIONS IN HIGH SCHOOL ATHLETIC DEPARTMENT. And after that — the two local radio stations. Maybe the city TV station.

And money, of course, I told myself blissfully. Barrels of it. New uniforms, new hockey fields, Gatorade, and tennis court resurfacing.

A few early birds straggled in, grumpy, sleepy, barely acknowledging my presence. They took a paper without glancing at it, adding the sheets to the bottoms of their piles. Another kid just brushed by me, rolling his eyes at the suggestion that he should carry one single burden more. And then with a burst, the whole student population merged, shouting, yelling, pushing, laughing, tracking in snow and slush and mud.

I passed out papers as fast as my fingers could separate the sheets. At the far door, Jonathan was swamped. I saw him divide his sheaf and enlist a friend of his to pass out the other half.

Half that quickly found its way to the floor. Most people seemed to have fingers so numbed by the cold that they could not close around anything so flimsy as a sheet of paper.

"They're like puppies," said Jonathan, during a lull, surveying the littered foyer.

"Puppies?" I said.

"Paper trained. Look at all the mud our position papers have absorbed."

Susannah and Chrissie arrived together, in a hurry as always, because they do their homework in the hall before class each day. I handed over my papers and they frowned, looking suspicious, but they accepted. I think mostly because we were in public, and they believed, as I do, in supporting the team. And I, however upsetting I had become, was part of their team.

I could feel them cringe, thinking of all the trouble that was to come from Tory's latest foray into rabble-rousing. I don't know what they expected to read — vicious remarks about Mr. Giametti's complexion, maybe, or libel about Dr. Chafee.

But as their eyes drifted unwillingly down my page, their foreheads wrinkled, their eyes narrowed. They froze into reading position: books leaning against their ankles, scarves falling from their shoulders, boots dripping. They read, and then reread, our entire position paper. When Susannah looked up, it was with a very different expression. "There's a lot here, Tory," she said uneasily.

Chrissie said, "I guess I didn't realize how *much* is wrong. In so many things. In *everything*."

I was exultant: This time they weren't disturbed over me — they were disturbed over the athletic department!

Some of the kids in my French class came by and of course said, "Merci beaucoup, Veeky" — Tory doesn't make it in French, so five hours a week Victoria becomes Veeky.

Jonathan and I laughed when the kids wiped their feet on some of our papers.

I should have been upset, but I wasn't. The school seemed to divide quite naturally: the interesting kids, the ones with get-up-and-go, read the paper and reacted. The dull, boring kids who never did anything, anyhow, not in class, gym, music, art, or anything else, didn't read the paper at all.

Jason Eames (the one who called me Miss Brownie Points U.S.A.) came by. "Tory," he said waving my paper, "this is actually a rather decent little collection of thoughts, all told."

I cared about as much for Jason's impression as I did for an alley cat's, but I thanked him anyhow.

"It's garbage," said Aaron. "She's making an Ice Age out of an ice cube."

Jonathan only laughed. "At least you know that your favorite No Bake can cook up a storm, Aaron."

Aaron left immediately, lest anyone else accuse him of having a favorite No Bake.

Two teachers paused, looking puzzled. For a moment my heart thumped erratically. I was going to be in trouble now. Jonathan just smiled and gave them each a position paper. Jonathan doesn't care what the teachers think, I realized. So why do I? Somewhere deep inside me is a good little girl who says, "Yes, sir," and does her share. Nice little girls don't do this. Any minute now the teachers will slap my palm with a ruler and send me home to Mother for a remodeling.

But the teachers didn't miss a beat talking about homework corrections and failing grades; they didn't even glance at the paper. Probably thought it was advertising another bake sale.

And the next person to put out his hand to receive a paper was Kenny Magnussen.

He looked perfect, of course.

I glanced down at myself. The emerald green blouse that had seemed so striking this morning suddenly felt garish. The jeans seemed uneven and the shoes gawky. At least I knew my hair was fine. "Hi, Kenny." I was impressed by my two words. First time in two weeks I had spoken to the boy I loved, and I didn't scream, "I adore you, Kenny, where have you been?" I hadn't flung my arms around him or kissed him eight hundred times. Just a casual, "Hi, Kenny."

What a woman, I thought. What control, what poise. What a waste, not to have Kenny sewed up.

Kenny took the paper without touching my fingers, and I felt the omission like a physical pain. "What's this, Tory?" He glanced at the paper and I glanced at him. What do I mean — glanced? I *studied* him.

This is a year for sweatbands, bandannas, ribbons, and barrettes. In another example of

123

continuing sex discrimination, Dr. Chafee thinks hair decoration is marvelous on girls, but he hates it on boys. Kenny had obviously been wearing a sweatband. Knowing the standards of fashion at Lockridge, it could have been a folded bandanna, a piece of shirt, or even a scrap of towel dripping thread in little ravels. Dr. Chafee is always making the assistant principal go out and confiscate sweatbands, like handguns. You see a lot of boys walking around with a circular dent in their hair from recent sweatband pressure.

"You just had your sweatband taken into custody, I see," I said. I longed to run my fingers through his hair and return it to its normal soft, floppy state.

Kenny smiled. The intensity of his smile was like a match, and I was a waiting pool of oil. I flamed, wanting him. It seemed as if his smile actually gave off light, like the sun. Kenny. Sunshine. Laser beam.

I shook myself.

"It's my halo," said Kenny. "Chafee wanted me to show the world."

I believed it. Angels would have to come in the shape and size of Kenny Magnussen. Preferably without robe and wings. Just pure Kenny.

Ferris materialized, waving position papers and mittens. "Tory! How could you do all this without even calling me? I feel so left out. I take two days off to visit my father, and you attack wrestling teams, interview

Giametti, and start a publicity committee with Julie, of all people."

"I would have called you," I said, "but the operator didn't have your father's new listing yet."

"They're putting in the phone tomorrow." We hugged each other. She looked so well put together. Not strung out, the way she'd been for so many weeks. I was so glad for her: to be past the draining worrying and be able to pick up the pieces and be happy again. "Can I pass out some papers, too?" she asked.

Kenny had vanished. How could someone so large and lovely just disappear like that? He'll come and go like a new TV show, I thought. One night I'll flip the channel and he'll be there; and then for weeks — silence. "I'm out of papers, Ferris," I told her.

"You can have half of mine," said Jonathan to Ferris.

For the first time Ferris realized that Jonathan and I were doing this together. Her eyes lit on him joyously, and then traveled back to me, and then very meaningfully back to Jonathan. I blushed. I never blush. My complexion is as dependable as my hair. But now I could only stand there being completely embarrassed.

Ferris smiled contentedly to herself and took half of Jonathan's papers. Then she handed them to *me* and said, "Keep up the good work, Tory. I'll go do the stairwell with Rah-Rah."

I felt like a Christmas tree, with my green blouse and my scarlet cheeks. I looked away from Jonathan, but there was no one coming to give out papers to.

"Rah-Rah?" said Jonathan, questioningly.

"That's what we call the cheerleaders. Rah-Rahs."

"You better find a nicer way to address Julie now that she's part of your team," said Jonathan.

The final bell rang. We had to go to first-period class. "Thanks, Jonathan," I said.

He handed me his leftover papers and took a while doing it. "Anytime, Tory."

I blushed a second time.

It came to me slowly (during French, when in my opinion everything is slow) that the whole thing is to have a team.

If you go out there and face the world alone, people are afraid. They don't want to stand up there next to you, and maybe look silly, or make a jerk out of themselves, or get into trouble. It would feel like one person playing football.

But once you have a team, you're official. You're printing up material. *Then* they fall right in line.

In English the teacher, Mr. Feldman, said, "You know we've been studying books and essays that changed the world. Tom Paine, Harriet Beecher Stowe, Henry Thoreau. It might be worthwhile this morning to take a look at an essay put together by Tory Travis."

"If *Tory*'s going to change the world," said Aaron, "I think I'd like to get off."

Mr. Feldman laughed. "She's not ready for the world yet, Aaron, don't panic. But she may change Lockridge High. All it takes is one person, you know." He looked at me. And his expression was a funny mix of glad and grieving. Like my mother, I thought suddenly. As if he thinks of pain when he thinks of changing things. "One determined person," said Mr. Feldman sadly.

I could make nothing of his sadness. That morning was so triumphant. No Bake Travis disappeared from Lockridge Senior High as mysteriously as she had arrived, and in her place was a heroine.

It was like sunshine — like going to Bermuda in February: it was heaven. I basked in the attention.

In chemistry Andy actually agreed to listen to the teacher in my honor and Jonathan declared himself willing to hold a beaker.

About four minutes into class, the loudspeaker came on. Dr. Chafee.

Now, Dr. Chafee never makes announcements. I mean, does a man of his stature waste his precious time telling students that Bus B is going to leave five minutes late? Certainly not. A principal delegates that sort of drudgery.

I wondered what sort of vital thing would bring Chafee before the mike? Perhaps a nuclear attack.

"Tory Travis," said Chafee's voice, "please

report immediately to my office."

The chemistry teacher smiled a little, as if she had been expecting this. "Don't worry about a pass, Tory," she said gently.

All of a sudden I felt terrifyingly young. What did all these grown-ups know that I didn't? What was the combination of pride and pleasure, of grief and pain, that they understood and I didn't?

It's nothing but a meeting with Chafee, I thought. What can he say?

"Tory Travis," repeated the loudspeaker ominously, "report immediately to the principal's office."

He's not asking for anyone else, I thought. Not Gwynne, not Mary Cat, not Julie, not Dusty. Just me. It's a good offense, though. Catch her alone. Gang up on her. Keep her separated from her team.

Jonathan said very softly, "You want me to go with you?"

"No. No, thanks. I'll be fine." I felt sick.

"I feel trouble," said Andy. "Something painful. And lingering. Lighted splinters beneath the fingernails, perhaps."

"Shut up, Andy," I said.

"Hurry up, Tory," said the chemistry teacher.

There were three chairs in Dr. Chafee's office. Mr. Giametti was overflowing from one of them and Dr. Chafee was relaxing in the other. Courteously they motioned me into the third.

I wanted to swagger a little, toss off a "Hi there, guys," but I was too tense. I couldn't manage a greeting at all. They'll suspend me, I thought. There are probably laws against passing out position papers without the principal's approval. My mother'll kill me.

"Tory," said Dr. Chafee quietly, shaking his head in sorrow. "Tory."

He was able to put an entire lecture of disappointment into my name. "Yes, sir?" I said. I was quaking inside.

"Tory, this is an excessive reaction to some very small things," he said, tapping my position paper with his pencil.

"Small?" I said. "But —"

He glared at me.

I swallowed. "The school budget gives $96,000 to the boys' athletic department," I said, almost whispering, "and only $23,500 to the girls'. That's not a small difference."

"Twice as many boys as girls participate," snapped Mr. Giametti.

"Then the biggest difference should be twice as much," I said. "Lockridge spends four times as much."

"But Tory," said Dr. Chafee, "where do you think this money is going to come from? Do you seriously think the citizens of this town are going to vote for a tax increase?"

Not if they were all like my father. "No. I think that you can rearrange the spending of the money you already have so that —"

"No," said Giametti. "We can't."

"Like basketball coaches," I said. "There

are *more* girls in basketball than boys. But the boys' coach gets paid eleven hundred dollars more than the girls' coach and that's —"

"Tory," said Giametti, "there are maybe seventy-five — at the most a hundred people at your basketball games. They don't even buy tickets. They just go. At the boys' games we draw three to four hundred spectators. They buy tickets and soft drinks and popcorn. The boys earn about five thousand dollars a year in their basketball games. And you girls — why, you have to have those bake sales of yours."

I could have strangled him for being so dense. As calmly as I could I said, "But Mr. Giametti, if we had eight o'clock scheduling, too, then we could charge for our tickets also, and we could earn money ourselves and —"

"Eight o'clock games are out of the question," said Giametti.

"Why?" I cried.

Chafee began raining things on me. Hurling them at me. He took every single item on the position paper and showed me how it would cost too much to do that and it wasn't possible to do this and I was just plain wrong about that.

"Tory," he said gently, "you must learn to take one day at a time."

They were talking to me as if I were suffering from a severe emotional disorder. "If you take one day at a time, all you do is survive. I want to win," I said.

"Tory, Tory. That's very immature. We

certainly expect better of you, of all people. It's not whether you win or lose, is it, Tory? It's how you play the game."

"But winning counts, too. Otherwise why play at all?" I countered.

"But you *are* playing on a winning team, Tory. So what's your beef?"

The arguments circled around me like an infinitely superior basketball player. I kept having the feeling that I was giving the wrong answers, saying the wrong thing — playing, somehow, into their hands.

But I couldn't get a grip on their arguments fast enough.

You know how the last fifteen seconds of the fourth quarter, if your team is sixteen points ahead, the coach will put in the junior varsity to give them experience? And you know how the first thing they do is lose the ball, because the other team isn't good enough to beat *you*, but they can whip JVs any day?

That's how I felt. Like an eighth grader going out on the court for the first time in a big game, cocky and excited — and losing the ball in the space of an instant and watching the other team score. That sick, lost, defeated feeling because you're inexperienced.

I knew that I was going to cry. The tears were like a rain cloud about to burst. It was my honor at stake — the men who understood versus the silly little girl who didn't.

And they won. I wept. In silent triumph Mr. Giametti handed me a Kleenex. I hated him, but I needed the Kleenex. "Now let's see a smile, Tory, honey," said Giametti.

He was my elder. My teacher. A man. And so I smiled at him. He and Chafee were delighted with my smile.

And that's the victory, I thought. There's something about a girl meekly smiling that makes men happy. They like my smile even more than my tears.

All my life I wil be expected to run the bake sale with a smile. No whining, Tory. Our fine, fine girls don't whine. No complaining, Tory. Smile and do your duty. Finish your share, have no tantrums.

So be a good girl now, Tory, and give us a smile.

And what does being a good girl mean?

It means giving things up. It means never fighting.

Dr. Chafee and Mr. Giametti loomed over me like people I could see from under the water: shimmering, changing shape, growing viscous. But there was nothing else to do. I had done every single thing I knew of. And I'd lost. When you lose a game, no matter how stupid the referee's calls are, you shake hands.

So I smiled at them, and accepted defeat, and left the office with my little blue late pass twisted in my palm.

E<u>leven</u>

"It's over," I said to Mary Cat.

She stared at me, her funny cat hair sticking up around her beautiful oval face. "Over?" she repeated.

I told her what had happened in Chafee's office. "We can't do anything more. They boxed me in. There's nothing more to do."

"It sounds awful," she said, and she put an arm around me. I could have leaned on her the rest of the afternoon, feeling dreary together, but Mary Cat drew herself up, smiled at me, and said cheerfully, "Well, kid, I guess that's that. Good try. You were right to go that far, but I guess that's it. So. The game against Kennedy is tonight. Put your energies into that instead."

My mother, I thought. Mary Cat is just like my mother. Never dwell on it. Steer clear of it. Smile and pretend everything is just fine. "See you in a few hours," said Mary Cat happily, and she went on down the hall, half loping, a curiously graceful walk only Mary Cat could do. And I thought: If we had eight o'clock games, the boys might lose some audience and some income and some status. That's why Chafee and Giametti won't hear of it.

Julie and Gwynne came flying down the hall, eagerness written all over them. "Forget it," I said, and I explained.

"We can't do *anything*?" said Julie, shocked.

"But I thought the pen was more powerful than the sword," said Gwynne. "I really thought if we published, it would impress people."

"It impressed them all right," I said. "Enough to tell us to shut up."

Julie said vaguely, "I have a thought somewhere."

"You probably lost it in your pom-pon," said Gwynne.

"Go bite your fingernails," said Julie. She made me walk off down the hall with her, so Gwynne couldn't hear her next sentence, and she said, "I do sort of have it in my pom-pon, Tory. What I'm thinking is . . . we needed more spirit behind that."

"Oh, Julie, come on."

"Really! We needed some sort of formation. A way to shove it down their throats, the way I shove cheers. We needed screaming."

"They're doing the shoving, not me," I said gloomily.

Julie frowned and looked thoughtful. "Well," she said at last, "if I get it together, I'll let you know. Because I still think —"

"My God," said Gwynne, joining us, "you *still* think, Julie? Does that mean you have thought in the past and plan to think again in the future?"

I left them to their sarcasm. They had nothing to offer me and I had nothing to offer them.

"You tried," said Ferris, "and that's the important thing."

I didn't like her reasoning. Trying wasn't nearly so important as succeeding.

"You can relax now," Ferris explained. "You did the right thing."

How did she expect me to relax when the right thing hadn't gotten me anywhere? I said, "But Ferris —"

"Oh, Tory, drop it! We have to play Western tonight, and another game tomorrow. And that's the most important game of the season. If you go into that game with broken rubber bands we'll lose."

It's Mary Cat whose rubber bands always break. Then her hair falls in her eyes and she uses that for an excuse if she misses a basket.

But Ferris was right. I went into the game with broken rubber bands and we lost. Fifty-two to fifty. The kind of score that eats you like acid, because it's two lousy points, and you could have gotten it yourself — and won.

I missed seven baskets. *Seven.*

It was an away game, and we didn't have that much of an audience. But everyone I knew was there. Including my parents, who rarely make away games. I could hear my mother screaming — and she never screams. *"Go, Tory!"* And Tory would miss another basket. And I could hear Susannah's mother shrieking, *"Lockridge, get it together!"* And Tory would miss another basket.

We trailed by those two rotten points from the first quarter and there was nothing we could do to break it. Mary Cat evened the count once with free throws, and then Chrissie managed a steal and an easy lay-up, so we were ahead two at halftime, but we fell behind again and we didn't catch up.

So we lost to Kennedy. Which meant losing the regionals.

Because of me.

We retired to the unfamiliar locker room. It seemed to me that the other girls were changing at the opposite end of the room from me. Mary Cat was crying. With her funny hair and her puffy eyes and blotchy cheeks she looked awful. Her senior year. She ha′ wanted to be captain of a championship team. To go out with trophies.

Thanks to me she was going out with nothing.

Giametti had been right. I'd lavished all that time and effort on stupid essays and paper pushing . . . and the morale of the team caved in and my own concentration went up in smoke.

Missile struggled for a decent thing to say: bolstering things that coaches are supposed to come up with to make you feel better about a loss. I sat staring into my towel. It was white. With thousands of tiny loops. I could pull them all out, I thought. That would kill some time.

"Well, girls, you'll be seniors next year," she said. "You'll have more experience. You'll —"

"I won't be," said Mary Cat thinly. "This was my last chance."

I put the towel over my head as if to soak up sweat, but it was soaking up tears instead. No wonder my mother had not wanted me to fight. No wonder the English teacher had looked sad about what I was doing. They had known. All the hurt inside me. And even worse — the hurt I'd done to other people. They had known it would come.

"Hey, listen!" cried Susannah. "We still get to celebrate. My mother's having us all over for a slumber party in our family room and has she got a treat for us!" Susannah delivered this in tones that implied at the very least that Mrs. Fargo was flying us all to London for the evening.

Why did I have to fail so publicly? Other people were content to fail quietly and neatly. Muffing a flute lesson here, missing an essay question there. Me, I had to fail in front of an entire school with my position paper; fail in front of an entire faculty; fail in front of my parents; and fail for my team.

Oh, God.

"Terrific," said Peggy, and she really seemed to think it was. "I love slumber parties."

"I've got tattoo paint," said one of the girls. "We can paint pretend tattoos on each other."

"Oh, disgust," muttered Chrissie. "Strictly for sick minds."

"And svelte bodies," said Ferris. "I've always wanted a wiggling dragon forking its tongue down my arm."

I didn't go to the Fargos. I went home alone and lay in my bed crying on my back, so that the tears ran into my ears and my hearing got soggy.

The boys didn't win their championship, either, but they got a dinner given to them by the Rotary Club . . . *because we're so proud of our boys,* said the Rotary president, his picture in the paper shaking hands with Dusty Lang.

Shame and defeat were like layers of clothing I could not take off. Winter wore on as winter does: gray and raw and cruel. "Nothing!" I said to Ferris. "I accomplished nothing. I even lost the game for us. I am truly nothing. A zero!"

"Now, Tory," said Ferris.

"That is not helpful!" I snapped. "Now, Tory," I mimicked her. "Now, dear. Now, now, now, now —"

"Shut up," said Ferris. "And if you're very quiet, I will tell you what I have learned so far this year."

I glared at her.

"It won't take long," said Ferris softly. "I didn't learn much."

I smiled unwillingly.

"I learned that to most of my friends my personal troubles were just a big bore. I nearly lost every friend I had, with all my whining and moaning. So I will tell you, Tory, what you were too polite and kind to tell me."

I looked at my fingernails. My polish was chipping. I was going to have to remove it.

"Tory," said Ferris very gently, *"shut up."*

I could hear the hot air leaving the heat vents and the distant hum of thruway traffic. I could hear my own heart beat and the faint shuffle of my homework papers shifting. I said, "Okay."

Twice my mother came in at night to rub my back. Another time she shampooed my hair for me over the sink. I have washed my own hair since I was eight or nine years old. Having a scalp massage was really wonderful.

She began packing my lunch for me before

I got up in the morning. Little special treats appeared instead of the usual three cookies and an orange.

But we never talked about it. We never said, "What went wrong?" or "Why did you give up?" or "How much does it hurt?"

Maybe we thought it would hurt even more if we talked.

My whole short-lived crusade disappeared in less than a month, but inside me the month swelled like a tumor. It was hard to see or think of anything else.

Two weeks and two days after the passing out of the position papers, Kenny bumped into me in the hall. "Hi, Tory," he said cheerfully.

"Hullo, Kenny." I had gotten over the worst of my self-consciousness. I could look people in the eye again and not flush with shame.

"I've been looking for you," he said.

"Oh," I said, because I had given up ever trying to say anything meaningful.

"Want to see a movie tonight?"

He was asking me out. Kenny Magnussen was asking me out. I said, "Sure."

"There are four playing."

"Two of which my parents won't give me permission to see."

"And one of which I saw last week."

"I guess we know where we're going then," I said.

The passing bell rang and we were going

in opposite directions. "I'll pick you up at six-thirty," said Kenny.

"I'll be ready."

And he sped off to his class.

I stood the way you stand when you've almost had a fatal accident; when a driver almost killed you, or you almost killed him. You get through it and then your kneecaps dissolve and your calves start to hurt. A dreadful coppery taste fills your mouth and you feel weak as a flu victim.

Kenny had shaken me up like milk and chocolate ice cream: made me into something else altogether.

I was even having a hard time breathing, thinking of it. I didn't lose him, I thought. He asked me out again.

Joy swirled through me, twisting my heart and my thoughts, making me laugh and then shiver with delight.

Kenny likes me. In spite of it all.

I sat through my next class writing the tiniest imaginable K.K.'s in the margin of my paper, until I had long columns of them. Then I embellished the columns with K.K. cross rows, until I had ornate Greek-style caps. Finally I constructed a whole Greek temple from K.K.'s. They looked like tiny, crooked bricks.

Kenny, I thought. I'm going out with Kenny.

I spent French usefully. I decided what to wear.

* * *

We got to the movies with five minutes to spare and there was a long, long line. If I'd gone with Ferris, we would have moaned and groaned. Walked up to check out the front of the line. Exchanged complaints with everybody we knew. And then gone back to the end of the line to wait it out. I hate not getting what I want. I'd always rather hang in there than surrender.

Not Kenny. He said calmly, "Line's too long. We'll go to the late show instead. Come on. Let's get ice cream."

And of course at the ice cream parlor, I could not make up my mind between two new flavors (cookies 'n' cream and almond marshmallow chocolate), and there was also my eternal favorite, butter pecan. You would have thought Kenny never once had difficulty deciding what to choose from a four-page menu. "Fudge ripple," he told the waitress, and then the two of them looked at me with frowns as I dallied. I picked cookies 'n' cream just for something to say, and of course the instant I said it I knew that I really wanted butter pecan. But I said nothing. Kenny was looking at me. *Don't bring up athletics,* I reminded myself. I cast around for something to say. "Did you see that new television series with all the police chases?" I said.

I couldn't believe I'd uttered that. I hate talking about television. What could be more boring than exchanging what you remember of TV dialogue?

But Kenny picked this up enthusiastically. Yes, he'd seen it, but it wasn't going to be a favorite. *His* favorite —

Kenny could really tell a story. He didn't have a boring line in him. I found myself laughing idiotically as he repeated the comic scenes for me and imitated the heroes. Instead of hunting through my head for anything to say, the words spilled out of me, and out of Kenny, and we tossed conversation back and forth the way I'd always wanted to toss kisses. "Time to go," said Kenny, astonishing me, because I thought we'd barely arrived.

"Oh, Kenny, let's skip the movie," I said. "Let's just keep talking."

Kenny stared at me. "But the movie is what we planned," he said, reaching for my hand.

If I put us on a graph, I thought, I'd be leaping narrow points and low, sinking valleys. Kenny would be a straight line. In total control.

I could not imagine Kenny seething as I had: bubbling like hot lava and overflowing onto innocent people. Kenny would always plan before he moved. And he didn't even move very much. It wasn't just his smile that was condensed: All his motions were efficient and well thought out, as if he disliked squandering energy on anything but the most vital moments.

I could not decide if I envied him or not.

All I knew was, when he held my hand,

and then slipped it around my waist, nothing mattered except being there.

I kissed the hand I was holding. I didn't even have to think about it, or worry over doing it. He drew his hand gently away, found the back of my hair, and we came together tenderly for a kiss.

Spring came in spurts. A day of warmth, a week of freeze. A moment of green. Then a stretch of steel and gray.

"Like my emotions," I told Kenny, but he didn't understand.

Kenny made a real effort to bump into me in the halls. Literally. He loved coming up behind me and nudging against me, gently shoving, half kissing, until my back was to the corridor wall and he had me cornered. "Oh, hi," he'd say, sounding surprised. "What are you doing here?"

And we'd both giggle and rush on to the next class.

After school and on weekends, we crowded our lives with each other. It was easier to fit Kenny in than fighting the athletic department. It felt better, too. Less failure.

And yet, we were so often at opposite points of the graph. Me at a high or low. Kenny on his even straight line.

When I got my driver's license Kenny could hardly tolerate it. He hated sitting in the passenger seat. "I'll go to the baseball game with you only if I drive," he would say.

"You drive going and I'll drive coming," I'd offer.

He'd accept. But he didn't like it. He liked me in the passenger seat and himself in the driver's seat.

I took over all the errands at my house. I'd go to the dry cleaners or the drugstore or the post office anytime. I loved everything about driving: steering, signaling, watching the road, gauging the distance and the speeds and the turns.

"You get so physical when you drive," complained Kenny.

"What do you mean?"

"You get too involved," he said. "Even the way you look into the rearview mirror. You're so bright-eyed and interested you'd think there was a rock band bus behind you."

"If I drove around bored and dull-eyed," I pointed out, "we'd have a crash."

"Just drive," said Kenny. "Don't make a big thing out of it. You always have to make a big thing out of stuff."

All his references to the athletic thing were like that — sideswipes. I learned not to bring up the subject. It just made him tense and me miserable.

I didn't try out for softball. I was afraid of being on a team again so soon. I still had all this anger simmering in me, and I was afraid I'd explode again and ruin things, for the team, for the school. Certainly for me.

I hoped that Kenny and I would reach the stage where I could tell him some of these things: share the anger and the frustration. But we didn't.

Still, Kenny and I went to most of the games. Boys and girls both. Until I got to know Julie I never had any use for cheerleaders. I just made sure to sit where they wouldn't be jumping around and blocking my view. I screamed when I felt like it, not when they led it. But now whenever I met her eyes I felt obligated to yell with her.

"Give me an *L!*" shrieked Julie's squad.

"L!" I screamed. I thought, What did she mean about needing more spirit? About how we could have won if we'd just had a formation and some screaming?

"Sit down," said Kenny. "You're going to tip me over."

"Oh, Kenny, don't be such a lump. Yell with me."

"Give me an *O!*" howled Julie.

"O!" I howled back.

"You're going to get a sore throat. Just sit down and relax," said Kenny.

What is all this about relaxing? I thought. Why am I dating a boy who wants me to relax? "How can I relax when we have three men on base?" I demanded.

"Give me a *C!*" Julie shouted at me. I gave her a *C* and I thought about spirit and formations but I didn't think of any solutions.

*   *   *

146

At the shopping mall, when I was peacefully looking at shoes and bothering no one, I had the misfortune of being interested in the same pair of shoes as Mrs. Chafee. "Well, well, well," said Dr. Chafee, smiling. "This is Victoria Travis, dear," he said to his wife. "A fine, fine girl. Tory's calmed down a lot this semester, haven't you, Tory?"

"That's what adolescence is all about," said Mrs. Chafee, patting me. "Finding maturity."

I held the shoe and seriously considered making a hole in Mrs. Chafee's head with the heel, but maturely, and with great calm, I walked away without damaging either one of them.

He would agree with Kenny, I thought. The whole world wants me to be like Kenny. A straight line on the graph.

Everywhere we went, I bubbled too much for Kenny's taste and he sat around too much for mine.

"If I were lacking school spirit," said Kenny irritably at one of the girls' softball games, "I wouldn't even come, would I? I'm here, aren't I? Stop vaulting around and stomping and screaming. *Please?*"

"It's more fun this way," I said.

"It drives me crazy."

I gave in. I always gave in.

"Good," said Kenny approvingly. "I like a girl who's calm."

T*welve*

It was one of those late spring days where the weather surprises you by being cold and chill, when the sky looks too soft and the grass has begun to green and the daffodils and forsythia have turned to gold. Kenny and I were parked by the city lake. He had the heater on, but mostly we were keeping warm with body warmth, which is definitely the best kind. A mother and her little boys were trying to feed the ducks, but the ducks weren't interested and no amount of coaxing and crusts could bring the ducks to shore.

"Chrissie and Susannah are going to coach Little League this summer," I said, snuggling against Kenny.

"Oh?"

"It takes a lot of patience. The seven-year-olds don't try to pitch. They have a big rubber tee and hit the ball off that, to give them a better chance. Susannah asked if I could help."

"Don't."

"Why not?" I ran my fingers over his face. I love his face.

"It'll take up too much of your time," he said. My fingers crossed a frown. I erased it with my palm.

"I have to do something this summer or I'll be bored stiff. And this would give me a chance to see if I'd like to teach gym myself. Or be a coach. Right now, Kenny, I don't even know if I actually like little kids." I watched the two boys chasing ducks and wondered if I would enjoy spending my days with that age. Probably not.

"You're going to get that job at Laurel Hills Nursery," said Kenny. "That's heavy labor. Moving all those bales of pine needles. Digging up those shrubs. Forget the Little League. You won't have a shred of energy left if you do that, too."

"Oh, go on. I have tons of energy. They could harness me and solve the energy crisis."

Kenny gave me his sexy smile. "I'll harness you," he said softly. We kissed so long that when we stopped, the mother and the kids and even the ducks were gone. "I believe a person should conserve strength," said Kenny. "Not use up too much at one time. Don't do it, huh? There won't be anything left for *us*."

"I get enthusiastic about things," I said.

"It's more fun that way, Kenny. I think there's something wrong with your philosophy. You never — emotionally, physically, or even financially — use up too much of yourself at one time."

He looked irritable. "You yelled so much at the game you couldn't talk to me the next day. You got so worked up about some discriminatory thing you read in the paper you couldn't string together a coherent sentence."

"If I sat around conserving my energy, I'd never get anything done," I said, equally irritable.

"You'll never get anything done, anyhow," snapped Kenny. "So just relax and stop whipping around trying to accomplish things."

"Are you referring to my position paper, Kenneth Magnussen?"

"Oh, don't get so prickly."

"Answer me!"

"Will you calm down?"

"No! You accused me of not being able to accomplish anything. I want to know what you mean by that!"

"I mean that you are like a person rowing with one oar. You can use up your whole life that way, and you'll just go in circles. I think you should use this summer to look around and think about —"

"I'd be bored out of my mind," I said through my teeth. "And I did accomplish some things. They're resodding the hockey field. They wouldn't have done that if I hadn't forced the issue."

"I doubt it. The parents of the girls on the field hockey team complained, too, and *they're* the ones who forced the issue."

"You make me sick!" I yelled. "Why do you have to knock what I do? Why can't you respect the idea of trying to do something?"

"I do respect it. I think there's a limit, though, and you've passed it."

"Limits, limits, limits," I shrieked so loudly that two joggers halfway around the pond turned to see what the commotion was. Kenny closed his eyes with fury. That was how he expressed fury. With his eyelids.

I flung myself back on my side of the car and Kenny sat motionless where he'd been all along. After a moment he started the engine.

"You drive the way you live," I said. I tried not to say the words because I knew I'd regret them, but I'd wanted to say it for weeks and the words came shooting out like bullets. "Carefully. Efficiently. Methodically. *Boringly.*"

"I suppose you'd like me to drive like a stunt man and take you home through people's backyards?" he said.

"No. I'd rather be the driver. I don't see why it's my lot in life to be the passenger."

Kenny's jaw tightened but he said nothing.

"Say it!" I demanded. "Go ahead. Say it. *Boys drive. Girls are driven.*"

Kenny stopped in front of my house. He didn't turn off the motor. He didn't look at me. I got out of the car and when he didn't speak, I slammed the door hard enough to damage the chassis and stomped into the house.

And that was the end of Kenny.

I cried for days.

It was a good thing I had Ferris. "I don't see how Kenny and I could have split up so completely over one little thing," I said to her mournfully.

"Little! You two had absolutely nothing in common. There wasn't one shred of your personality that matched his."

"Our lips matched."

But forgetting Kenny didn't come any more easily than forgetting the position paper, or the confrontation with Giametti and Chafee, or the horrible lost game. I still lay there at night, staring up at the ceiling, trying to think my way through it all, and getting nowhere.

My mother came in to rub my back. Lately it was the only form of communication we had. She said, "Tell me, sweetheart. I know I haven't been much good to you recently, but try me again. I think I've improved."

I was face down in the pillow. I said, muffled, "Kenny."

"Him," said my mother shortly.

"What do you mean — *him*?" I said.

"I didn't care for him. He didn't have the right attitude toward you."

"What do you mean?"

"He was jealous of you."

If she had said Kenny was a Soviet spy, I could not have been more astonished. Kenny — jealous of me?

"Tory, you set the whole school on fire. Kenny couldn't do that. For all his looks and brains and skill, Kenny is just another kid. You're not. You're special."

I couldn't take the idea in. We had split because we were so different, not because of Kenny's jealousy. Surely!

"Sometimes," said my mother, "I think most men are jealous. Your father is an exception. But men have so much competition that doubling it is pretty scary. And you, Tory, even scared men thirty years your senior. Dave Giametti and Ray Chafee."

I had never heard their first names before. Dave and Ray. It made them distinctly less frightening.

"Doubling it?" I said.

"If they let the girls have what the boys already do, they'd have twice as many people trying for the same slots."

She's admitting it, I thought. She's not pretending anymore. She's come around to saying it aloud. The boys have more and they always have.

"I love you," said my mother in a thick, choked voice. "I didn't help you at all. But it was because I knew you'd get hurt and I didn't want that."

I had been hurt. But my mother had suffered for years, and I had only been aware of it for weeks. "I love you, too," I said.

It was a year for coming in second. Both the boys' baseball and the girls' softball teams placed second in our region. The school celebrated what there was to celebrate with a bonfire late one night. I went only because I had to get out of the house and have some action.

People had collected scrap wood and pallets to make a heap that must have reached twenty feet. Chrissie had brought marshmallows and we had a good laugh over that — the fire department wouldn't let us within fifty feet of the fire!

The flames soared far into the dark sky. Thousands of tiny sparks drifted like stars overhead, caught by the wind and pulled into wonderful swirling patterns until they went out and became ash. The firemen unrolled a rubber hose and circled the huge fire, spraying the grass where it threatened to light and wetting down trees as they got hot.

The cheerleaders ran out in front, screaming and clapping, their cute little skirts flared and their hair bouncing like TV ads for shampoo. I had to admit — they had spirit.

The flames leaped and danced. There were huge thrusts of spun sugar of orange and yellow.

I was mesmerized. I had never seen fire like that: pure flame, reaching, eating, devouring. It was beautiful.

The crowd screamed for school spirit and the moment I screamed, I had some again. We screamed for victory, and I felt a little of it. We screamed for captains and we screamed for letters and by the time Dr. Chafee began his little speech into the mike I was feeling the celebration in my bones.

So I lost this year, I thought. So what? Some of us are winning. Next year will be my year, Missile says.

Mr. Giametti began yelling out the names of each boy on the baseball team. "Rob Disario!" he bellowed, and the firemen pulled the sirens and the cheerleaders screamed and the flames sang to the sky. "Steven Wisnicki!"

I got so caught up in it that I felt ancient. Primitive. Like some distant ancestor, worshipping the stars and the fire, dancing around the black stones and praying over the glowing embers. The night was so black, the fire so bright, the shouts so brave and yet so puny in the vast, open air.

Mr. Giametti finished up with the boys' team and said, rather casually, as if it bored him, "And also the girls' softball team did well." And he unplugged the mike, and the firemen aimed their hoses on the fire and it was over.

Over.

Not one girl had had her own yell. Not one round of applause for Susannah, who was the captain, or Mrs. Ellis, who was the coach.

People pushed by me, still excited, leaping

over the ropes that kept us back from the fire, yelling good-byes to their friends, honking Morse code farewells on the car horns, loping over the pavement to catch up with families who had a TV show to catch.

The bonfire had been for the boys.

Girls could come, of course. We were welcome to celebrate their victory. We could cheer, stomp, congratulate . . . but what we were celebrating was them. Not us.

I stood in the shadows. The embers hissed and complained as the fire was put out once and for all. Dark, evil smoke rose in fat, suffocating, pillowy shapes from the dying flames.

I began walking home.

It was crazy, dangerous, and stupid to walk home in the dark. I had promised my mother I'd get a ride with one of the girls. And I could. Easily. Everybody was there.

But I didn't want any of them. I had to walk off my fury. Kenny's right, I thought. I go too far. There are limits. I have to relax.

And what is relaxing about being a second-class citizen?

I crossed a broad stretch of grass, black at night, and leaped a drainage ditch and walked along the verge. Tears began when the smoke irritated my eyes, and tears continued because I had no other solution to my problems.

The cars vanished down the main road and I walked alone down the lane toward my neighborhood. Trees rustled in the slight wind and something crunched behind me. In the distance I heard a dog yapping. I hate strange dogs.

"Tory?"

I almost fell into the drainage ditch. A voice from nowhere, whispering at my back.

"It's just me," said the voice. I had to feel the body to figure out who the voice belonged to, it was so dark. "Jonathan?" I said, amazed.

"Yup. Tory, you're crazy to walk home."

"You must be crazy, too, or you wouldn't be here."

"I'm riding with some other guys. They said they'd wait while I chased after you. Tory, it must be three miles to your house and not a streetlight till you get to town. Come on, ride with us."

I would rather spend the night in the ditch than ride home with celebrating boys, I thought.

Jonathan hugged me. It was a soft, comforting hug that lasted and lasted. It was the hug of a friend. How strange that of all my friends, it was Jonathan who was there.

The dog yapped again. I like dogs I know, but little yappy dogs that go after my ankles in the dark make me very nervous.

Jonathan said, "I can *feel* you not liking the dog barking. Come on. Drive home with me."

"I should not be afraid of dogs," I told Jonathan. "A modern, twentieth-century woman should at least be afraid of something reasonable, like nuclear war, instead of *dogs*.

My parents keep wanting to buy me a dog. So I'll get over this."

"Why should you get over it?"

"Because it's stupid."

He shrugged. "I don't like tennis or asparagus and I figure I can get through life fine. Some things you just don't like."

"But you're not afraid of asparagus," I pointed out. "I feel so dumb being afraid."

Jonathan laughed. "Tory, you have to be the bravest, most poised person I have ever known in my life. Name one person besides you who could stand up to principals and coaches, wrestling teams and a whole student body? You wade into the enemy day after day, like some sort of guerilla squad commando, and never show a single scar."

Me? Brave?

"Come on," he said. "They're waiting."

I walked reluctantly with him back to the car.

"Hey," he said, "forget who's driving. It's a car, right? Take advantage of somebody for a change. Be the taker, not the giver."

"It shouldn't work that way."

"Well, it does. What you have to learn is, you have to learn how to shrug."

I had heard that line before, too. And I didn't like it one bit more from Jonathan.

_T_ hirteen

"Dad?" I said.

"Yes, honey." He was reading his paper, which he does very intently, so Mother and I always feel guilty when we speak to him during newspaper hours.

"If I wanted to keep my fight against the school athletic department going, where do you think I could go next?"

My father literally flung his paper to the floor. I stared at its separated sections in amazement. When I looked back at him, he was grinning at me. "I cannot think of anything on God's earth I'd rather have you do," he said.

"You're kidding."

"Oh, Tory!" He laughed and hugged me. "I was so proud of you when you took that on. But when you gave up, I didn't feel I ought to push you. It's your fight, not mine."

"I didn't need a push," I said. "More of a helping hand."

"Ah, Pumpkin," he said, looking almost ashamed. "I'm sorry. I could have helped. I just kept remembering your piano lessons and how we shoved them down your throat and I didn't want to make the same error — have you hate me, night in, night out, forcing you into something you'd rather have dropped."

"Why did you make me take piano lessons?" I said. "I *hated* them. And I'm so totally *not* musical."

"Oh, we thought you'd learn self-discipline. The art of practice, or something. We should just have waited till you took up basketball."

We need to talk more, I thought. This whole family needs to talk so much more! We have all these ideas and thoughts about each other but we keep them private. If we'd just share it, how much better it would be! I said, "Then you do think there's something else I can do?"

"You've hardly begun," said my father.

I waited, but he didn't go on. "'Well?'" I said impatiently. "Like what?"

"You have to remember that what we're talking about is money. You wrote a nice little position paper, but you missed the important part. You wrote of emotions, of girls versus boys, of locker rooms and uniforms, picnics and programs. Forget all that."

"But if I forget all that," I objected, "what is there to complain about?"

"The only ally you have is that law," said my father. "The Title IX law. And what it says is, the school has to make equal expenditures regardless of sex. So you have to research the Lockridge budget. Get it broken down to the tiniest expenditure you can find. See how the boys really compare to the girls. If fifty boys play basketball and fifty girls play, too, then they should have equal funds for equipment; their coaches should be paid the same; their transportation and uniforms and supplies should have equal allocations. And don't stop with Lockridge and don't stop with basketball. Check every intramural sport and check the neighboring towns as well. I don't know whether our neighbors do better or worse than we do, but you'll need the facts for ammunition."

He sat with his hands clasped between his knees, his eyes bright and excitement tucked in behind his sentences. I could not remember him looking at me that way before. He wants this as much as I do, I thought. Probably for different reasons.

"But, Dad," I said, "who would I fire on?" He didn't seem to understand that I had already tried the principal and the athletic director and they'd said no.

My father straightened up and laughed shortly, dismissing that problem. "Forget Giametti," he said. "Forget Chafee. They're just employees. Small potatoes."

They didn't seem very small to me. Especially not Mr. Giametti.

"They have eleven bosses," said my father. "The school board. Go for the school board."

That night as I lay on the same bed, staring at the same unseeable ceiling, the simmering anger was gone. In its place was a strange, carbonated excitement. I knew now what Julie meant. *Spirit*. It was something inside you. A flame with the wind behind it. A bonfire that burned in your heart and kept you going.

Jonathan was carrying his cello. I am always surprised at how graceful he and the instrument appear together, although the cello is in a hard case and is such an awkward, heavy thing. When he has the cello, Jonathan always has an air of being enviable: as if really terrific people are always seen with their cellos, and those of us without a cello just don't quite cut it. "Hi, Jonathan."

"Hi, Tory. How are you?" He stood the cello on its little spike and the two of them waited for me to go on.

"I'm fine, thanks. Fine enough to feel like taking something on."

Jonathan grinned. "You're like a weed under the driveway, Tory," he said.

"How insulting! Today I feel like a daffodil or a tulip and you tell me I'm a weed."

"We used to have a gravel drive," said Jonathan. "It drove my mother crazy, because the weeds were always coming up through the stones. No matter how much she weeded, or sprayed with herbicide, it wouldn't be long before these little shoots of green would appear. So my father said we'd put tar down, and we did. And by the end of the second summer, one patch of weeds was so strong it had bumped out the tar, and a little green sprig had worked its way up to the sun."

I stared at him, and the little blonde hairs on my arms prickled. How could he know me so well: Jonathan, who was barely an acquaintance? How could he know I wanted the sun — the wins — the bonfire?

"Taking on what, this time?" said Jonathan. His smile was still there. It was a quiet smile. A person enjoying himself on the inside. "The same? Something different? Or variations on the theme?"

How musical he made it sound! As if all I had to do was play the right tune on the right flute. "Variations," I said. "I want someone to go with me to Kennedy High and Western High to find out their athletic budget figures."

"Sure," said Jonathan, nodding. "The last paper was pretty weak in the statistical department. But we won't want to go to the schools. We'd have to make explanations to the school officials and word would get back to Chafee. I'm sure it's public record and available at the town hall."

He was so matter of fact. Not like me.

Kenny is right, I thought. I do have to calm down. I have to keep right on trying — but trying calmly. Instead of getting emotional and threatening visiting wrestling teams and ripping up Invisible Brownies, I have to be a fact finder.

"How about this afternoon?" said Jonathan. "My cello lesson is in Lynford, not far from the town hall. We can look up Kennedy and Western. If you can tolerate a half hour of string playing, we'll drive on over and do Lynford before supper."

That, of course, was the day I ran into Kenny. I know why ancient people believed the gods are capricious and manipulative and even cruel. Because they are. Because Kenny said to me, "Tory? Want to go for a drive this afternoon?"

Oh, Kenny, I thought, and my knees melted. I adore you. And today I'm going to fight the athletic department, and I can't tell you that, and I'm going with Jonathan, and you think he's a wimp, just the way I used to. I'll have to fib.

I tried to think of a really good lie that would make Kenny ask me for another day, but Kenny misunderstood my hesitation. "You can drive," he said, which from him was the concession of a lifetime. "I have my father's Corvette."

He knew I loved that car. He knew nothing excited me more than feeling that heavy engine, the surge when I shifted gears and the thrill of controlling such a sleek, tough car.

Kenny's been lying awake, too, I thought. He's willing to compromise. He'll meet me halfway. Forget half. I'll take ten percent.

We were standing next to my locker. At the same instant each of us tired of being upright and leaned our shoulders against the gray metal, so we were now slanted and several inches closer.

I could postpone Jonathan. All I had to do was tell him so. He'd be nice about it.

But today I had the courage, and today I had the right partner for that research. Another day it would be different. If I waited, it might not work. "Kenny, I'd love to, but today's impossible," I said. "Could we make it Thursday?"

"I didn't know you had anything today," he said, as if knowing my schedule intimately was one of his priorities.

"It came up very suddenly," I said, and against all my better judgment, I began telling him what I was doing.

I knew him well enough to read expressions that would have passed before as merely an eyebrow, or a lifted chin. Oh, smile at me! I thought. Love me.

But I had said all the wrong things, and I knew they were wrong even before I said them. I tried to redeem it by saying, "Why don't you come along, Kenny?" even though I knew he got along with Jonathan about as well as I did with Mr. Giametti.

"I guess I can't work that out, Tory," he said. "But let me know if you ever feel like a drive, okay?"

"Okay," I said, and it was horrible, because we both knew we were just being polite. He wouldn't offer me another drive, and I wouldn't suggest one.

I wanted to fling myself on him and forget everything else, drive off in the Corvette and never worry again about anything except Kenny.

But I didn't.

Jonathan's cello lesson was hardly something to endure. He was so good that even someone as nonmusical as I am was thrilled. His teacher yelled at him steadily, shrieking that Jonathan had not practiced, that he had no sense of line—and Jonathan would just nod slightly and play the phrase again and the teacher would give him a smile so tiny I could barely detect it, but I could see that they were both satisfied now.

Jonathan liked being yelled at by his cello teacher the way I liked it from Missile: it was to push him forward, to build him up, to show him how. It was coaching.

You get cemented into your own hobby and don't notice other people's. I would have said a cello and a basketball had nothing in common, and yet there was so much. You had to care, you had to practice, you had to love your instrument, your coach, your team, your goal.

"I've never seen you look daydreamy before," remarked Jonathan, when we walked into the Lynford town hall. Lynford has two high schools, each slightly bigger than our single school. Kennedy and Western.

"I've been thinking about cellos and basketballs," I said.

"Hmmm," said Jonathan dubiously, and I was glad that at least there was one thing he didn't immediately understand. I would not want to be as transparent as glass all the time. "Excuse me, sir," Jonathan said to an irritable-looking plump man walking by. "Can you tell me where we would find the school system budget records?"

The man stared at us suspiciously. "What for?" he said.

"School paper," Jonathan told him. "We're not really sure how to start, sir, and we'd be very grateful if you'd point us at the right filing cabinet."

The man snorted. "Not my department," he said, and I thought he would stomp off, but he led us around the corner and pointed up the stairs. "Second door."

Up the stairs.

Second door.

The sign protruding from the wall read: FISCAL PLANNING. We walked right in and a secretary frowned at us. "There must be something about working for the city that makes people irritable," Jonathan murmured to me. I smiled and repeated his words to ask the secretary for help.

"Oh, sure," she said. "No problem. What year do you want?"

I thought. "The last three," I told her, for no reason except to sound official and school paperish.

Five minutes later we were seated at a table in the hall perusing the last three years of the athletic budgets at our rival schools, Kennedy and Western.

Jonathan had a pad and pen and started to take notes, but I shook my head. "You stay here looking busy," I said. "I'm going downstairs to the copying machine in the hall."

What would have been frightening on my own was a snap knowing that Jonathan was along. There were even two adults waiting in line behind me to use the copier and I was able to smile and say I'd be done in a moment. Not that I was doing anything wrong — it was just that I felt like a trespasser, gathering secret facts as a secret weapon.

But they noticed nothing and spent the minutes gossiping about somebody they suspected of creative bookkeeping, whatever that was. I went back to Jonathan and we returned the records to the secretary with profuse thanks.

"We'll have to do the other schools another day," said Jonathan, looking at his watch. "How big a rush are you in, Tory?"

"Not too big. I think we have another week."

"Till what?"

"Till the annual school board meeting for the public to discuss next year's budget."

Jonathan began laughing. It was a private, sort of breathy laugh. Very personal. And then he kissed me. But that wasn't very personal. It was more a sharing of enjoyment. "There's bound to be quite a crowd there," he said. "Always war over the school budget. But there won't be any kids. Just you and a few hundred parents and irate taxpayers."

"I'm going to convince them," I said.

"I love it," he said, laughing again. He held the door open for me and I thought, It *is* "it" that Jonathan loves. The action. The determination. Not me — but "it."

Ferris was wrong about Jonathan having a crush on me. He's too self-sufficient for that. He just likes being part of the action. "What's creative bookkeeping?" I said. I was having a funny rush of disappointment. As if somewhere inside me, where I hadn't even known I was thinking about it, I'd been hoping Jonathan had come because he liked me.

"Stealing," said Jonathan. "I'll come the night of the meeting. And of course Gwynne and Dusty will. Mary Cat. Beth. Julie. And you can probably talk Ferris into it. You want me to round up anyone else?"

"No, because I don't want to alert Chafee

and Giametti. I'm not even going to tell Missile. I don't want her involved."

Jonathan nodded. I could see his brain lining up the action like so many notes on the musical staff.

It's interesting how some people don't seem that good-looking until they're your friends, and suddenly you like every freckle, every curve of the cheek, and every angle of the bones. He's very handsome, I thought, and I could no longer tell if he really *was* handsome, or if he had become that way to me because I liked him now.

The next day I was headed for the school bus when Kenny was backing his father's Corvette out of its slot and heading home. He saw me and waved — but Jonathan was with me, and the wave was short and not followed by a smile.

Jonathan noticed nothing, not even the car. How could someone not notice a classic red Corvette? Especially when driven by a classically handsome preppie like Kenny?

Kenny turned the corner and disappeared like a red arrow behind thick, dark fir trees. I climbed on my bus and Jonathan climbed on his. I felt alone, but strong.

I studied the papers every day, and every day when there was nothing my father and I exchanged sections and long looks.

One week before the end of school it was there.

* * *

ANNUAL SCHOOL BUDGET
MEETING

The Lockridge school system's budget for next year will be up for public review Wednesday at 7:30 in the City Hall Annex. Taxpayers and parents are urged to make their views known.

Fourteen

"You're going to do what?" said my mother in a thin voice. Her hand was tight around her coffee mug and she pulled her robe around her with the other hand, and the lace gathered and pinched at her throat.

"I'm going to present a show to the school board meeting. Jonathan and I have copies of the last three years of athletic budgets for our high school and four others. We've drawn up comparison charts for every single sport and for all the basics, like uniforms and coaching fees. We're putting it on the overhead projector and I'll give a talk while he changes the transparencies."

She sipped her coffee. Please be on my side, I thought. Please don't get shook. I'll be okay.

She said, "I want to hear it. Stand over there by the piano and rehearse it for me."

I pushed my chair back and got up. I

cleared my throat. I felt stupid and awkward already, and it was just my mother, not the school board and a few hundred taxpayers. "Well," I began. "I'm going to — uh, point out some, you know, problems we have. In the gym. I mean, the athletic department. Mostly they're girls' problems. They're unfair."

My mother looked at me in disgust. I flushed. "I better start over," I said.

"I think so, too."

I started over. I said, "Well."

"Tory, no. When you give a speech you address the people present. You say, 'Ladies and gentlemen, thank you for letting me speak tonight.' Then you introduce yourself. You say, 'My name is Tory Travis.' Then you say who you're speaking for. Like, 'I am here tonight on behalf of the three hundred female athletes at Lockridge Senior High School.' "

"Two hundred and nineteen, Mom. There are two hundred and nineteen girls at Lockridge in competitive sports."

"Out of how many girls altogether?"

"Out of five hundred and seventy-seven girls in the whole school."

"Which is what percent?"

"Roughly one third."

"How does that compare to the other schools?"

"Parsons has only twenty percent active in intramurals and Western has thirty percent. In spite of the fact that Lockridge is smaller by —"

"Enough," said my mother. "That was good. You knew that by heart. You'll have to memorize the rest, too. Never look at a paper. It makes you look like a bumbling amateur. Now what order will you be going in?"

"Order?" I said.

"You can't just pour out facts like water from a faucet. It has to be logical and easy to follow. Perhaps you could take basketball and follow it through all five schools. Now, you'll need to practice in front of a mirror so you can catch any mannerisms that will irritate the people watching you. You need to rehearse with Jonathan so he changes the transparencies at the right moment. . . ."

Every day when my mother got home from work, she got herself a Coke, sat down in the softest chair in the living room (to rest her back after a day of typing), and nodded at me. Using the piano for the school board and the couch for the audience, I'd give her my speech.

"No," she'd interrupt. "Talk that fast and nobody will understand a thing. You're teaching dunces who know nothing about your subject. Be slow with them. Repeat the important things."

At school we kept it quiet. Just the few of us who had been involved from the beginning. We didn't know what Chafee and Giametti could do to stop us, but they'd surely come up with something and it had to be a secret. It was most odd keeping it from Missile, when it was her arena, so to speak.

"And your mother's rehearsing you each night?" said Mary Cat. "You are so lucky to have such a supportive family, Tory. My mother would disintegrate from worry. She can hardly live through basketball games, she's so panicked about how I'll do."

A supportive family, I thought. Yes, I do have that. And supportive friends. I looked at Julie, whose feet were dancing although she was sitting down, studying the transparencies, and I thought of cheers and spirit and bonfires. You don't really have to have those, I thought. You can have friends and parents and they're just as good.

"This stuff needs to be illustrated," said Gwynne. "I mean, it's all very well to talk about lousy tennis courts, but we need photographs of them."

"Great idea," said Jonathan. "Unfortunately we have less than forty-eight hours left."

"Just get them from the archives," said Julie.

"What archives?" we all demanded.

She looked at us as if we were retarded. "The yearbook," she said. "It's part of photography class to take shots of the school grounds and the kids and the action around the building. They have stuff going back for years."

Gwynne let out a war whoop and hit Dusty so hard he fell forward. We all giggled insanely. "Simon's a good guy," said Dusty.

"He'll help us, I'm sure. I feel safe in telling him what we need the stuff for. He's very anti-authority. He'll like doing something that the principal *won't* like."

We rushed down to the art department and cornered Simon. I don't know why nobody calls the art teacher by his last name. He's just Simon, to everybody. He grinned when we told him what we wanted. An hour later we had photographs: the torn nets, the puddled water, the ruined hockey field, the dented lockers. "But you don't want photographs," said Simon. "You want slides, so you can show the entire audience the photographs on a projector."

"Slides?" I repeated dismally. How could we possibly get slides done so fast? If only I'd thought of this earlier, so we could have planned ahead!

"No problem," said Simon. "I'll make them up for you."

"I love you, Simon," said Gwynne.

"All the girls do," agreed Simon. "Now beat it. You've given me an awful lot of work to do in a very short time."

Tuesday night my mother said, "Well, your speech is perfect. Now. What are you going to wear?"

"I don't know, Mom. I guess my good jeans and my cotton knit top. The one with the trim around the keyhole at the neckline."

"Absolutely not. No jeans. A dress."

"Mom! I don't even own a dress!"

"You have that lovely wraparound skirt, the deep blue one. It makes you look very tall and slender and feminine."

"But I —" How to tell her that that felt strange? I never wore dresses. I'd feel peculiar, even hypocritical, wearing a dress.

"If you go in there like Miss Jock, they'll say — oh, well, a girl like that, what do you expect? But if you look the way they want *their* daughters to look — why, then, they'll have to think again about the thirty-three percent of their girls who are active in sports, won't they?"

My mother ironed the skirt for me. It's important to know that neither of us ever irons. I knew we had an iron, and I even knew where it was, but I didn't actually use it. The family rule is — if you have to iron it, don't buy it. I stood there, watching her iron my skirt and I began to cry and we looked at each other and *she* began to cry. Little drops of her tears fell down on the fabric and sizzled when she passed the hot iron over them.

She set the iron down carefully — we use it so little we're afraid of it — and turned to me and hugged me, biting her lips to keep from crying again, and she said, "I'm so nervous."

"*You're* nervous!"

"There's so much at stake, Tory." She laughed shakily. "Oh, honey. At your age I never could have — Let's face it. At *my* age I couldn't do this."

She ran her finger down my cheek, tracing the tear lines, and she hugged me fiercely and whispered, "Whip them, Tory."

Jonathan called a few minutes later. "You ready?"

He knew I was. We had rehearsed everything, including the slides we didn't have yet.

"I called Simon. He's got it all done. He says to skip lunch tomorrow and come to the art room and he'll help us with the order and so on." His voice was something like his cello: smooth and musical and sure. I love his voice. It is like a symbol of Jonathan.

". . . certainly rehearsed enough. So I don't have any qualms," said Jonathan. "They'll be impressed right out of their sweat socks."

What a nice person he is, I thought. Calling for last-minute bolstering.

"Hang in there, Tory," he said, and the phone clicked.

It rang, still in my hand. "Tory?" said Missile. "What's this I hear from Simon down in Art?"

"Come to the school board meeting," I told her.

"Tell me what you're up to, Tory, please?"

"We've decided it's our project and we'll go it alone and take responsibility for whether it flies or sinks, Missile."

There was a silence. I didn't know whether to apologize or say good-bye. Missile said, "Well, Simon gave me a few clues. I'll be watching, Tory old girl. No fumbles. No fouls. I want nothing but perfect shots, hear?"

"We've had some heavy practice," I said.

"It's different at a real game. You face the opposition and sometimes you panic."

"The opposition doesn't even know I'm coming."

"Ah, Tory," said Missile, and I could feel her emotion on the phone, although I was not entirely sure what the emotion was. "Good luck, kid. See you tomorrow."

"My voice will crack," I whispered to Ferris. Already I could feel the preliminary prickles of fear running up and down my rib cage.

"Be grateful," she said. "If I were doing what you're doing, I wouldn't even *have* a voice."

"I'll trip on my way to the microphone," I said to Mary Cat.

"You could carry a basketball," she suggested. "Dribble it around a little for special effects."

We giggled nervously. There were seven of us sitting in the second row: me, Ferris, Gwynne, Dusty, Jonathan, Julie, and Mary Cat. Not the front, where I would feel totally exposed, and not the back, where I'd actually have to see the entire audience that was going to listen to me.

"Be calm," said Gwynne.

Jonathan laughed softly. "It's a world-wide conspiracy against you," he murmured. "Shoving calm down your throat."

My stomach shredded into thin, painful ribbons of terror. There was nothing funny about not being calm. "You do it, Gwynne," I said. I can still back out, I thought. This isn't official. I'm not on the agenda or anything.

I glanced behind me. With six minutes to go before the meeting began, the large room had collected maybe a hundred and fifty adults. I could see my parents. They were as nervous as I was. Missile slid in to sit with them, and their heads came together for a conference.

My entire hand was shaking. Even my wrist quivered.

"Look at that," said Gwynne happily. "Three reporters, all with cameras. And both radio stations. Good, I called them, spelled your name, and everything. We want all the coverage we can get. Too bad there's no local TV station. Now relax, Tory. And don't make any mistakes."

Oh, that was relaxing.

My teeth shivered. My tongue got fat. My lungs collapsed. At the front of the room, raised about five inches, were two large tables and eleven huge, comfortable chairs behind them. The school board drifted in slowly, looking very school board memberish. The type that dresses perfectly, talks perfectly, holds perfect jobs, and contributes to the civic welfare from a sense of duty.

Not simple-minded, wimpy, and inarticulate like me.

I had to go to the bathroom. I was going to throw up or have diarrhea or both.

Ferris said, "My gosh! I had no idea there'd be so many kids here. Of course, the rumors were flying, but I didn't think anybody would actually come."

Julie turned in her seat to look. "It's everybody! But how did they all know? I thought we were keeping it top secret."

I swiveled very slowly, as if in a neck brace, and looked. Row after row was packed with high school kids. Chrissie and Heidi, Iowa and Jason, Susannah and Kenny. . . .

"Tory, everytime I think I've seen everything," said Jonathan, "you do one thing more to impress me. Where did you find the time to organize all of them to come?"

Kenny detached himself from the others and walked our way. He slid into the third row and came in sideways until he was right behind me, and he sat down, putting his hand on the back of my seat. "I thought it would look better with some support from the rest of us," he said. We stared at each other. I whispered a thank you, but it didn't really come out.

"I count sixty-three kids, Kenny!" said Mary Cat. "You must have called half the school to get this turnout. And I swear Chafee and Giametti don't know anything about it. Look at them, twisting in their seats and getting upset and whispering back and forth!

This is the last thing they expected!" She clapped her hands with glee. "Honest-to-goodness student participation."

"How did you do it?" I said at last.

"Threats," said Kenny, and we all collapsed in stifled giggles. We got some irritated looks from the two school board members who had come in.

"You think I do nothing but lie around and stay too calm," said Kenny. "You think I'm so objective I'm just a slab of rock. You're always saying I never cheer. So I'm proving you wrong. I not only brought the cheering squad, I trained it."

I couldn't cry. It would spoil my makeup. I squeezed his hand for a moment and a moment was all I had.

"This meeting," said the chairwoman of the school board, "will please come to order."

They discussed things that no sane individual could ever care about, and they discussed this stuff for hours. Motions were made and seconded and amended and put in the record. I would have unraveled my entire sweater sleeve if Jonathan hadn't taken my hand and held it very firmly in his. My hand was dripping with nervous perspiration. It must have been like holding a damp, warm sponge. But Jonathan didn't seem to notice.

The chairwoman was a pompous woman. Mrs. Bartoli. We had the feeling she was on the school board so as to hold a gavel in her hand, not because she cared about the school.

"Is there," said Mrs. Bartoli in her most affected voice, "any new business before we approach the budget?"

I took a very deep breath and got to my feet. I could feel every one of the people sitting behind me. Staring. Wondering. Worrying. I said, "The students of Lockridge Senior High would like to make a brief visual presentation."

She almost refused. She drew herself up, exchanged an unreadable look with Chafee, and seem poised for a no — but she saw Kenny's crowd, and she saw the reporters perk up, and she didn't quite have the nerve.

"I can allot you ten minutes," she said sharply, "and no more."

Ten minutes! I thought. *That's half what we planned.* I checked my watch. Okay. I would do it in ten minutes, then. I walked to the microphone. The cameras turned toward me. My teeth started hurting as if they expected to be drilled. Mrs. Bartoli glared at me as if she was expecting anything from mud wrestling to nude dancing.

Jonathan rolled up the overhead projector and the slide projector. Mary Cat went to the corner of the room and pulled down the screen. Julie stood by the light switch panel.

I took the mike out of its clip and held it loosely in my hand. "Ladies and gentlemen," I said, and I froze. I literally could not remember my name. Eye contact, my mother had insisted. I used my time to make eye contact with everybody from Missile to Giametti and I remembered my name. "I am Tory Travis and I'm speaking to you tonight on behalf of the thirty-eight percent of the female students at Lockridge Senior High who are active participants in competitive sports." Don't rush, I thought. Just because you have only half the time doesn't mean you speak twice as fast. You'll just have to omit some things.

"We're going to discuss and compare the expenditures of Lockridge High, Parsons, Western, Kennedy, and Roosevelt Central in four important sports. We're going to see the dollar amounts spent on boys and girls in the same sport. We're going to see how Lockridge compares to its neighbors and to the rest of the state. We're going to examine the federal laws dealing with equality of expenditures and see whether Lockridge schools are conforming to the law."

I swallowed. It was hard, because I had perspired away all my fluids. My mouth was fuzzy. I can't deal with this! I thought. Jonathan lifted his chin at me in silent communion — *Go on, you're doing fine* — and Julie flipped off the lights, leaving me in blessed, anonymous darkness.

"The first chart is basketball," I said. "You can see that basketball is equally popular with boys and girls at all but Parsons. You might assume that equal amounts are spent per pupil, but you'd be wrong. Kennedy has *exactly* the same number of boys and girls participating but they spend 2.1 times as much on the boys. Roosevelt and Western are even worse, with 2.2 and 2.5 times as much money for the boys. Only Parsons comes close to being fair, with 1.8 times as much spent on boys as girls. But now look at the column for Lockridge."

Jonathan's pointer slipped across the chart and was magnified on the screen. The audience gasped audibly and murmured. "Exactly," I said. "At Lockridge we have six more girls than boys participating in basketball. But Lockridge spends 3.8 times as much for the boys."

I let that sink in a moment and went on to break the figures down. "Look at what Lockridge pays its basketball coaches. The boys' coach receives nearly twice as much as the girls'."

I looked at my watch. I had done only basketball and used up six of my ten minutes. "Jonathan," I said helplessly, "the slides, please."

He had already realized the problem and was ready.

"There is no comparison for field hockey. Our school didn't offer this popular girls' sport this year." Jonathan showed a color slide of the field: It was a wonderful close-up. A girl's legs, her striped socks, her hockey stick, and the grass: tufts of it, a hole in the ground, an obvious, treacherous dip in front of her feet. "The field was not maintained. It was felt the boys needed the money more. Lockridge had to give up field hockey."

Jonathan flashed on a picture of a tennis court: smooth, sunny, well drained, the net taut and waiting. It made you ache to be out there, in your whites and new sneakers. I said, "The boys' court."

He pressed the switch and the next picture was another sunny day, but dank and shadowed behind the school maintenance buildings was an uneven, puddled court, its net torn and sagging. "The girls' court," I said.

The ten minutes were gone. For all our rehearsing we had not realized how much time would be consumed by how little. So many of my best facts and pictures and charts could not be used. I thought briefly of going on anyhow, but it would make an enemy of Mrs. Bartoli. Better to accept the ten-minute limit and hope it had had good effect.

Jonathan flicked off the machine; Julie put the lights back on. The audience coughed and shifted and blinked. I said, "I would like to quote you from a federal law called Title IX: *No person in the United States shall, on the basis of sex, be excluded from participation in, be denied the benefits of, or be subject to discrimination under, any education program or activity receiving federal assistance.*"

I swallowed one last cottony swallow. It was over. I was done. "Thank you for your time," I said, and I clipped the mike back and went to my seat on knees made of jelly.

court, smooth, easy, well turned, the out
fast and calling. It made you echo to be out
there in your whites and your sneakers. I

Fifteen

I had forgotten that people applaud for speeches. I knew they clapped for good baskets and good passes and for getting up off the floor when you've been hurt. But I had never made a speech and I had not realized that anybody would applaud.

I don't know where it began. I think with the kids — but by the time I turned away from the school board, half the room was clapping. As I sank into the chair next to Jonathan, the room was shaking with applause.

I didn't know what to do. In basketball either you keep playing or you sip water and throw a towel over your face. You don't have to acknowledge the applause — just enjoy it.

Jonathan breathed, "Perfect, Tory."

A voice like Missile's. Or his cello teacher's. *Perfect.* A word Jonathan would not use if he didn't mean it.

Jonathan squeezed my right hand and Ferris my left. Mary Cat and Gwynne were both hunched forward, with their hands tucked between their knees.

The chairwoman cleared her throat. "Order," she said testily. "Order, please."

The clapping died away, the talk ceased, and Mrs. Bartoli stood there looking annoyed. She looked at Chafee and he gave his head a slight negative shake.

No.

"They can't slide right over it," whispered Mary Cat. "Surely not!"

Mrs. Bartoli gave the assembly a tight smile, nodded as though dismissing the applause from the room, and picked up a sheaf of papers she'd carried in with her. They could not be papers that had anything to do with our presentation. She was going to move onto another subject.

It was like reading a shocking test score: when you studied hard, and were pleased after the exam, sure you're getting above ninety — and the teacher hands it back and you smile with secret pleasure at your brain power — and you have a sixty-eight.

Instantaneous icy shock.

Failure.

Nothing to do but swallow, check the smile for another day. So quick that failure comes! No preparation allowed.

You spend your whole winter and spring on something. You lose friends and make enemies. You turn it in your mind until your mind aches from the weight of it. You find friends and strategies, get spirit, get it done . . . and they ignore it. They dismiss the applause, and what does clapping matter, after all, unless you win the game? You get applause for a good basket, but if you're twenty-six points behind and there are only eleven seconds left in the fourth quarter, what does it really matter?

Even Julie could not have mustered a cheer at that moment.

And then one of the men on the board cleared his throat. I hadn't particularly noticed him before. He was quite old and I suppose I thought an old person would have old-fashioned feelings and not want change. "While Miss Travis was giving her presentation," he said — and he gave me a funny little salute with two of his fingers — "I was doing a little figuring on my note pad here. Now, next year's budget calls for an eleven percent increase for the competitive athletics division of our physical education department." He paused and looked out at the parents and taxpayers. "And every cent of that increase," he said softly, "is for the boys."

The audience reacted noisily. My skin prickled and Jonathan's hand moved in tension.

"Well," said Mrs. Bartoli, before she could lose control, "I certainly agree that Miss Travis had given us all something to contemplate. I am impressed by the amount of student and parental support shown tonight.

I can see that the board will definitely have to meet and consider a different funding arrangement. But now we must move on to *important* things. The math department has requested eleven new minicomputers. As you know, this is a new and vital field and one to which all our students must have access. May I bring to your attention the following. . . ."

Julie maneuvered her spoon very carefully up to her mouth. Since there were nine of us in a six-person booth (my parents, Missile, Kenny, Jonathan, Julie, Mary Cat, Ferris, and me — Dusty and Gwynne had gone off on their own), not getting chocolate sauce on other people was a top priority. "Well, old girl," said Julie, happily licking the drips off her spoon, "you sure did it this time."

"It was wonderful, wasn't it?" said my mother, crushed between my father and Kenny. "When you got to your feet the *second* time, Tory, after all that jazz on minicomputers, and requested that the school board make a public commitment to equity in spending, all the parents around us kept saying, 'Imagine a girl of sixteen with the poise to do all that!'"

"It was ex," said Ferris, who prefers the first syllable only of long words such as excellent, "truly ex, Tory."

I was squashed between Missile and Jonathan. It made me think of the backseat of her car, and the Burger King, where it had all begun for me. "You don't understand," I said. "Nothing happened."

My mother's spoon sagged halfway to her mouth, and little chocolate splats hit the Formica table.

"They're going to consider the situation," I said. "And that's exactly what they'll do, too. They'll consider it."

"Right," said Kenny. "And then they'll do something about it." He was directly across from me, and both of us were wedged forward, so that we were leaning into each other's faces and sundaes.

"I doubt it," I said.

"Oh, Tory," said Ferris irritably, "don't sit and sulk. It's time to celebrate. It was all so much fun."

"Don't you see that it doesn't matter if we had fun and Kenny brought everybody out in force and we were impressive?" I cried. "We didn't get anything done!"

"I don't believe this," groaned Kenny. "Where's all your famous enthusiasm and verve, Tory?"

And Jonathan, sitting on my left, put his arm around my waist. It wasn't a simple feat. He had to snake past Missile's waist to do it. His arm circled me comfortingly. Don't say something comforting, though, I thought. Please don't add to all this. Please let somebody understand! "She's right, you know," said Jonathan. "Nothing happened. It's not like a chemistry test, or a basketball game.

Where either you win or you don't. Tory's at war, and it's not going to be easy. It's not going to be a quick war. It'll be" — he hesitated, looking for the right phrase — "it'll be —"

My father supplied it. "A war of attrition."

"What's that?" said Ferris. She wanted us all to be happy and enjoy our ice cream.

"Fight after fight after fight," said my father. "Each side wins a few and loses a few, and finally one side just gives up and then the other side wins."

"But Mr. Travis," objected Mary Cat, "you make it sound as if this could go on for ages."

"It probably could," said my father.

The celebration — if there had been one — came to a halt. We sat, jammed in together, uncomfortable, inspecting our spoons, moving our cherries on top of our whipped cream, looking forlornly for the last walnut. "I think," said Kenny firmly, "that the whole thing should be shelved for the summer. It would ruin your summer if you kept agonizing over this, Tory."

Ferris said that was right.

Julie said Kenny had a good point.

My parents and Missile said nothing. They won't shove, I thought. Whatever I do, or don't do, they want it to be my choice.

Jonathan said, "It would probably ruin Tory's summer if she *did* shelve it."

Where do they come from — these people who understand? Why do the people I've known for so long, like Ferris, not really ever figure out what the score is? How come I didn't recognize Jonathan before? Why didn't I realize he was my kind of person? Why did I want Kenny, when Kenny knew nothing of me at all, and I knew nothing of him?

Jonathan knew me, inside out. Jonathan was so lean and relaxed and mature and —

And I'm crazy about him, I thought.

Kenny had brought me a team, yet he wasn't *on* my team. He'd helped in order to prove he wasn't a clod, and not because he believed in me or my cause. Kenny was a fine person and I was very grateful to him: He'd done a wonderful thing for me.

But it was Jonathan, literally and figuratively, who had held my hand and gotten me through.

My father said, "The next thing to do is for you and your mother and me to go talk individually to each school board member. We have to gather up all the statistics you didn't manage to use, Tory, and give them to the reporters from the radio and newspapers."

My mother said, "I was talking with Simon, the art teacher, Tory. He gave me permission to make as many copies as I like of the slides. The media people can use them. They'll need that kind of thing to print, to get people's attention."

Kenny protested, "But it could go on all summer!"

Missile spoke for the first time. "It's gone on all my life," she said. And she and my mother looked at each other, and there was a bond between them: eyes that met and felt the same pain and ached for the same ending.

My mother and Missile.

And me.

himself and her first times. It's been going
on all my life, she said. And she and my
mother looked at each other, and there was a
I don't know, there was a still and a ch
No

Sixteen

It was the kind of summer that hangs sus-
pended in the heat and seems to last forever.

The flowers in my mother's garden died
young from too much sun and too little rain.
We forgot what clouds looked like, and without our sunglasses on we looked damaged,
with white ovals around my eyes. I worked
eight hours a day at the nursery, selling
hanging baskets of purple fuschia and load-
ing bales of pine bark mulch into the backs
of station wagons. When I got home I was so
dirty my mother actually spread newspapers
for me to walk on. Some days I thought
vaguely of reading the newspaper before it
met this filthy end, but I never got around
to it. If nuclear war broke out, I would notice,
and nothing else seemed important.

Jonathan and I played tennis and swam in
the lake at the state park and ate at least six
thousand Dairy Queen cones, because we were

both soft ice cream addicts. We went to the mountains for the outdoor symphony concerts, sitting dreamily through the music while staring at the stars and thinking of each other.

And while we were busy, at the same time we seemed to be doing nothing except absorbing the sun's rays. We never talked about the athletic thing. We hadn't meant to shelve it, but July and August did it for us. My life condensed to seeing Jonathan, finding a second bathing suit, ringing up fertilizer sales, and taking showers so I was fit company for Jonathan.

I didn't even know what day it was when my father joined Jonathan and me out in the backyard. Jonathan and I were talking of nothing: getting his cello bow restrung, returning an overdue book to the library, having a blister on the heel. My father sat beside us — but not close enough to touch, because it was too muggy for that — and fanned himself with the paper. "It's here, Tory," he said.

"What is?"

I was watching Jonathan. He was wearing only his cutoff shorts, and he was so tan and terrific looking, spread-eagled on the grass because he believed the earth was cooler than the steps. It was impossible for anyone to come or go without leaping over him. Since it was too hot to leap, or even trudge, I was just sitting there drinking Coke and admiring him.

"The results of the school board meetings," said my father.

I actually had to think. School board. Meetings. What could that have to do with me? I let an ice cube slide into my mouth from my Coke and crunched it between my teeth, so that the frozen shards splintered soothingly down my parched throat.

"In the paper?" said Jonathan, raising himself up on one elbow. "What's it say?"

"It's a long article," said my father. "There are only two sentences that apply to us."

"Oh, good," said Jonathan. "Spare us the details."

The locusts shrilled. Mosquitoes whined. My father read: " 'Mrs. Bartoli also mentioned that due to Title IX requirements, the school board was forced to rearrange funding for boys' and girls' athletics for the coming year. As a result, the boys will have to manage without any dollar increase in funds whatsoever, while the girls have been given a generous thirty percent increase.' "

There was a long silence.

Long enough to hear things I didn't normally hear. Traffic on the turnpike, two miles away. A door slamming down the block. My mother's footsteps on the stairs inside.

The school board was forced, I thought. They didn't opt, they didn't choose, they didn't vote, they didn't decide. They were forced. I was the force.

I took the paper from him and read the two sentences myself, and then I read the whole article. My name wasn't in it. The open meeting wasn't mentioned. The arguments and the furor that must have gone on behind closed doors wasn't mentioned. Just — *the school board was forced.* . . .

I read the front page. It seemed to me something of vast and overwhelming importance should be there. The president was worried about Central America and the economists were worried about Social Security and the weather was going to stay clear and hot.

And in Lockridge, Tory Travis had forced the school board to increase the girls' athletic budget.

"Thirty percent?" said Jonathan, getting up and brushing the grass from his thighs. "That's a lot, Tory. I figured maybe ten percent. Maybe even nothing but — 'we're working on it, says Mrs. Bartoli.' " He took the paper out of my hands and read it over himself.

"You did it, Tory," said my father, in a matter-of-fact voice, as if he were announcing supper, or the need to put a few gallons of gas in the car before we set out.

Jonathan let out a yell of delight they could have heard at the turnpike exit and grabbed me in his arms and swung me around the patio and danced me around the pile of bricks we call a barbecue. "You did it!" he yelled. He kissed me three times: each cheek, and then my lips, and tossed his plastic cup (free with a large drink if you also buy a banana split) into the air to celebrate.

I did it, I thought.

My mother came out to see what the commotion was, and because I was busy reading the article again, trying to figure out what a thirty percent increase really meant, she hugged Jonathan instead and then the three of them hugged each other and then we all hugged and I said, "Don't wrinkle the paper."

My mother giggled. "We'll get more copies, Tory. We'll buy out the whole edition. We'll call everybody we know and ask them to clip the article. We might even wallpaper your room with it."

"It doesn't even have my name," I said.

"It will," said Jonathan. "I'll call the paper and the radio stations. They'll love it."

The phone rang and my mother went in to answer it.

"Knowing Chafee as I do," said Jonathan, "I bet he'll think of some way to get credit for this himself. The fair-minded, farsighted principal once again takes care of his dear, dear girls."

"Fine, fine," I said.

Jonathan looked confused.

"His girls," I explained. "They're not dear, dear; they're fine, fine."

Missile's car pulled into our driveway and she tumbled out, waving the newspaper, yelling, "Did you see it? Did you read it yet?"

Out the window my mother yelled, "It's

for you, Tory. It's Gwynne and Dusty."

"At the same time?" said Jonathan. "What do they do, split the phone in half?"

"Tell them to come on over," I yelled back.

Missile said, "Everybody ought to come. Let's call the team. I'll treat to pizza. This calls for a celebration."

"Now that they're finally going to pay you what you're worth, you're rich?" said my father, grinning.

Ferris and her mother drove in behind Missile's car, and not ten minutes after that Mary Cat and Julie, with their boyfriends.

I had not known how many people read the daily paper. Especially boring, stuffy articles about school boards in the second section. The phone rang constantly. My parents' best friends came over, as though there had been some adult cheering section I hadn't even known about. The next door neighbors appeared with their ice cream machine and their own homegrown raspberries. Simon came, and Mary Beth, and Missile's boyfriend, a man we'd heard about but never met, and he wasn't too bad, although not in my opinion good enough for her.

"Let's not have pizza," said Dusty. "I like steak better. And it's more of a celebration."

"May I charge this to you?" said my father. "There must be fifty people here."

Dusty admitted that perhaps steak was a little expensive. We agreed on hamburgers and hot dogs, and Jonathan's parents said they'd buy the sodas, and Missile said she'd do the chips, dip, and pickles, and Ferris and her mother took on rolls.

"I bet we get our laundry done now," said Mary Cat.

"If they fix the girls' tennis courts, I have first dibs," said Ferris.

"My mother's calling the papers back to make them interview you, Tory," said Gwynne, "and give credit where credit is due. Mom phoned me at the dry cleaners the minute she read the article."

"*The dry cleaners?*" said Jonathan. "What were you doing at the dry cleaners in August, and how did your mother know to find you there?"

"I work there," said Gwynne. "That's why I'm so shriveled looking. They boil me every day."

Dusty said, "You think that fire's big enough?"

We looked at the pile of bricks. Dusty had enough wood on there to roast a steer. The flames must have reached six or eight feet. My father attached the hose just in case and wetted down the grass around the bricks.

Jonathan's parents were back with the soda and five bags of ice cubes and paper cups, and everyone rushed for the card table where my mother was setting it up, and Jonathan said to me, "There it is, Tory."

"What?"

"The bonfire. The one you didn't get."

I looked into the flames and thought of all that had happened during this crazy year and I said, "Let's not get carried away. We're not equal or anything. It was only thirty percent."

Jonathan said, "It wasn't *only*. Don't say *only*. It was something special, Tory, and it was you."

The evening passed with laughter and talk, speculation and mimicry of Chafee, Giametti, and Bartoli. The dusk was hot and thick. Somebody brought marshmallows and we scoured the place for twigs and sticks and we toasted them over the coals. Jonathan did mine the way I love them: black, burnt, clinging to a charred stick. I toasted his the way he loves them: pale brown, hardly even warm on the inside.

Missile and my parents, her boyfriend, Jonathan's parents, Ferris's mother, and the rest of the adults sat jammed on the picnic table, having iced coffee. The kids hunched around the fire, jockeying for marshmallow space over the embers.

It was very late when I noticed that Missile had moved away from the fire and was lying in a soft patch of grass, staring up at the stars. I moved over beside her.

"Thirty percent," said Missile. "I can't get it out of my head. Like a hit song, going over and over inside me. They actually were forced to increase our budget by thirty full percentage points in one year."

In the dark her face was ghostly, removed. I looked up where she was staring. Stars and the winking lights of planes.

"It's an improvement," I agreed.

My marshmallow burned my tongue in a satisfying way: gooey and crunchy at the same time.

"The sky is good for heavy thinking," said Missile. "As good as a fire. Or the sea lapping the sand. Eternal."

"What are your heavy thoughts?"

Missile picked a thin blade of grass and put it in her teeth and she said, "It takes only one, Tory. One to struggle. One to keep going."

She blurred in front of me. Tears seemed to come for all of us. For we had all kept going. My mother, Missile, Julie, Ferris, Mary Cat. Each of us, in her way.

"There's more to do," I said, hating the thought, shrinking from it.

"I know. It's like winning the regionals. Now you have to go on to the states."

"But I can't do anything more, Missile," I said.

She took my hand, and the firelight danced on her eyes. "Nonsense," she said.

The tears were gone. There was nothing blurry at all. I seemed to see her and everything else more clearly than I had ever seen anything before. She was right. It was nonsense. I could do more.

And I would . . . with Jonathan cheering all the way.

Move from one breathtaking romance to another with the #1 Teen Romance line in the country!

NEW WILDFIRES! $1.95 each

- ☐ MU32539-6 **BLIND DATE** Priscilla Maynard
- ☐ MU32541-8 **NO BOYS?** McClure Jones
- ☐ MU32538-8 **SPRING LOVE** Jennifer Sarasin
- ☐ MU31930-2 **THAT OTHER GIRL** Conrad Nowels

BEST-SELLING WILDFIRES! $1.95 each

- ☐ MU31981-7 **NANCY AND NICK** Caroline B. Cooney
- ☐ MU32313-X **SECOND BEST** Helen Cavanagh
- ☐ MU31849-7 **YOURS TRULY, LOVE, JANIE** Ann Reit
- ☐ MU31566-8 **DREAMS CAN COME TRUE** Jane Claypool Miner
- ☐ MU32369-5 **HOMECOMING QUEEN** Winifred Madison
- ☐ MU31261-8 **I'M CHRISTY** Maud Johnson
- ☐ MU30324-4 **I'VE GOT A CRUSH ON YOU** Carol Stanley
- ☐ MU32361-X **THE SEARCHING HEART** Barbara Steiner
- ☐ MU31710-5 **TOO YOUNG TO KNOW** Elisabeth Ogilvie
- ☐ MU32430-6 **WRITE EVERY DAY** Janet Quin-Harkin
- ☐ MU30956-0 **THE BEST OF FRIENDS** Jill Ross Klevin
